The Golden Sword

Book 7
Marti Talbott's Highlander Series

By
Marti Talbott
© 2011 All Rights Reserved

CHAPTER I

ESSEN MACKINNON WAS hungry when he blew out the candle, set the holder down on the table, and carefully opened the door of his mother's well-hidden cottage in the forest. The darkness outside was as complete as the hurt in the boy's heart, and he had not realized how hungry he was until that moment. It was not his imagination, the sweet smell of cooked fish was true and when he looked, he could see the glow of a small fire near the edge of the river.

Cautiously, he crept closer, hiding his small frame behind one bush or tree and then another until, at last, he could see the silhouette of a very large man seated on a rock near the fire. The man's back was to him and the boy paused to more carefully look around. Where there was one man, there were usually others and from the abundance of aroma, it was likely the meal was being prepared for more than just one.

He knelt down and watched for a time. He could hear the rushing water in the river and the crackling of the fire, but he heard no other sounds and saw no one else. The man made no sudden moves, but from this vantage point, the boy could not see exactly what the man was doing. Essen had just begun to creep closer, when the man's voice broke the silence.

"Ye need not steal what is free, laddie."

Startled, the boy held his breath. He was certain he had been quiet enough not to be noticed. More importantly, how did the stranger know he was a child and not a grown man?

"Are you not hungry? Come, eat, I will not harm you."

Essen dared not make a move. Many times his mother warned him of vile things that happened to little boys, the worst of which was being sold into slavery and never being seen in Scotland again. Yet, the man's voice sounded kind and oddly familiar. That was impossible. They lived a considerable distance from their clan's village and very few knew of their existence. Essen's mother let no man near them and lately thought to kill one to protect their solitude.

It was the first time Essen had seen death and his mother visibly shook when the deed was done. She left the man in the woods, but the next day when they went back to tend the burial, the body was gone. It was possible someone else discovered the body, but she feared the man was not dead after all, and warned Essen to be especially careful. He heeded her words as he always did and even now considered them. Yet the stranger by the fire was not the same man, of that he was certain, for this man was much larger.

"Even when his heart is hurting, a laddie must eat so he will grow strong," said the stranger.

Timidly, Essen stood up. The glow of the fire highlighted his curly blond hair and flickered in his blue eyes. "Are you a MacKinnon?"

"Nay. Will you sit and eat with me laddie? 'Twill be glad for the company."

"You are alone then?"

"Aye."

Essen did not quite believe the stranger, and made a wide berth around the fire, until he could crouch behind another bush and look the man over. What he saw troubled him. The man wore a shirt and kilt of almost pure white.

"Are you God?"

The old man chuckled. "Hardly, I am Moran of Clan Larmont." He pulled two wooden bowls out of a cloth sack and set them on the ground. On 'Y' shaped sticks, one at each end of the fire, rested another long stick holding three large skewered fish. Careful not to burn himself, Moran lifted the horizontal stick and used his dagger to push two of the cooked fish into the bowls. Then he put the stick with the remaining fish still on it back, put his dagger away, de-boned one of the fish and set the bowl on a rock. "'Tis for you, laddie, when you are brave enough."

Still Essen hesitated. In the yellow light of the small fire, the man's face might well have been a pleasant one, but the shadows distorted it. "Do the Larmonts wear white?"

The old man shook his head, "Nay, Larmont colors are red and blue. 'Tis that my kilt...well, 'tis a long story, that one. My mother taught me to shear, spin the wool and weave the cloth, but not how to dye it. Have you buried your mother?"

Essen took a chance and stepped out from behind the bush. "Aye." Tears began to streak his dirty face. His MacKinnon yellow and blue kilt was frayed at the bottom, his shirt was torn and his hair was matted. "She was heavy."

"Aye, the dead are always heavy." Moran de-boned a fish for himself and began to eat. Between bites he said, "A lad must never cry, even when his heart is hurting. Tears cloud the eyes and he will not see danger."

The boy quickly wiped his tears away with his hands and took another step closer to the bowl on the rock. "She was naked."

Moran slowly closed his eyes, "I am grieved to hear it. Do you know the man what did it to her?"

He kept his eyes on Moran, took a last step forward, grabbed the bowl and backed away. "Nay."

"'Tis just as well. A heart filled with hate is a waste of a good heart." Moran watched the boy finally begin to greedily eat and remained quiet for a time. Then he said, "Tonight we will sleep and on the morrow, we will begin. I have much to teach and you have much to learn. You will be a good and fair man when you are grown, Essen MacKinnon, for you know the hurt a vile man can cause."

He marveled that the old man knew his name, few did. His mother put off going to the village for as long as she could, just to avoid men who approached and tried to claim her. It was her smile that drew men to her, Essen realized once he was old enough. One husband was enough and his mother had no wish to take another. Her smiles were for her son alone. Without fail, she made certain no one followed or knew where they lived, so how could this stranger know his name?

"Where might your father be, laddie?"

"Banished."

"I see. Do you know his crime?"

Essen was nearly finished with his fish and began eyeing the one remaining. "Nay, mother did not say of it." It hurt to talk about her and he had to push the urge to cry away. It hurt to wash her body, to put her in the shallow grave he struggled to dig, and to toss the dirt on top of her. When he found her deep in the forest, he took off his kilt, covered her nakedness and sat down to watch, but she did not take a breath and her skin turned cold. It had to be done, so he buried her.

Moran pushed the last fish off the stick, removed the bones and offered half to the boy. He was pleased when Essen accepted it and finally sat down on the rock, though he was careful to keep himself out of the old man's reach. "Are you listening, laddie? You need not fret, I will teach you all I know and then you will carry on the search."

Essen took a bite, swallowed and stopped eating just long enough to ask, "Search for what?"

"The sword, laddie, the golden sword. Some say 'tis just a legend, but 'twas my father who saw it. Nay, 'tis true right enough. I am an old man and my days are numbered, but you will find it, Essen MacKinnon, and when you do, you will find happiness."

ESSEN SLEPT OUTSIDE that night just as the stranger said, and only returned to the cottage in the woods the next morning to get the things he would need. He was not unhappy living there, indeed his mother's love kept him completely content. Yet, the old man offered adventure and it was time for him to taste it.

When he'd finished gathering his things, he moved a rock near the hearth and recovered the two gold coins she kept hidden there. Then he picked up her brush. Perhaps the fondest memory he had of her was the way she brushed her long, blonde hair and the smile she always turned to him when he could not resist touching the softness.

He stuffed the brush in his bag, put the bag over his shoulder and softly closed the door behind him, as though she were merely asleep inside. For a moment, he wondered if the whispers in his mind would go with him on his adventures.

When he returned to the river, the old man was gone.

Nothing remained, not a hint of a fire or any evidence that Moran actually existed. Was it nothing more than an unkind dream? For the first time since his mother's death, Essen felt completely alone and helpless.

Something near the river moved.

The speed with which the boy hid his sack and himself in the bushes surprised even him. It had to be Moran, he decided. Still, someone had murdered his mother and could yet be in the area. Again, the bushes near the river moved, and then a man stood up and appeared to be watching something in the water. It was not Moran, nor the man who killed his mother, of that he was certain. This man wore the colors of the MacKinnon clan. Essen remained hidden until the MacKinnon finally left the river and walked up the path toward the village.

Curious, the boy crept closer to the river. He saw a sack bob back up in the water, dropped his belongings and waded in just in time to grab it before it floated down stream. He hauled the wet, heavy woolen sack to shore, opened the strings and dumped the bodies of four bearded collie puppies on the ground.

Too many hungry dogs run in packs and kill children, his mother once said. It was good to be rid of them. Just now however, he did not see the wisdom in her words. There was too much death in the world to suit him and these puppies had not harmed anyone.

Suddenly, one of the puppies moved.

Elated, he opened his own sack, pulled out a plaid and began to dry the pup's fur. "Keep breathing, wee one," he whispered. "You shall be my dog." It was clear the puppy was too cold even after the fur was dry, so Essen opened his shirt and tucked the small life inside where his body could warm it.

"'Twill be a good dog," a voice behind him said.

The old man was back and Essen was greatly relieved. "Aye," he said, standing up and turning around. In the morning light, he discovered the old man had a pleasant face with auburn hair, a reddish brown mustache and beard, and smiling blue eyes.

"You did well, laddie, you did not let the lad see you. You did very well indeed."

"Will the pup live?"

"Not as long as you, but he's cheated death this once and will again. Name him Blue."

"A color?"

"Aye, should you need him but dare not call out, say the sky is blue."

"And he will know to come?" the boy asked.

"We will teach him to know." Moran began to gather wood and peat for a new fire. "Might as well wash yourself, laddie, whilst you are already wet. I'll mind the pup." He was pleased when the boy quickly handed him the dog and headed for the river.

ESSEN FULLY EXPECTED the old man to take him on an adventure, but such was not to be. Instead, they remained near the edge of the river. At night, he learned the cycle of the moon and how to know where he was by the placement of the stars, when the clouds did not hide them, that is. Essen was well aware of the short winter days when the sun barely rose above the horizon and the long summer days that kept the sky too bright to see the stars. Yet he did not know how to hold a torch near the edge of the river to attract fish for an easy meal. Essen most feared the furious gales that made the trees bend and threaten to fall on the cottage. The old man had no words of wisdom on that subject. There was little a man could do about such things.

During the day, while the birds chirped in the trees and an occasional rabbit hopped into their small camp, Essen learned to become a better hunter. He was too young and Moran's sword was too heavy to learn to fight sufficiently, but the old man fashioned a crude wooden sword just the right size and showed him the basics. More important than knowing when to slice and when to jab a sword, was learning how to outsmart his opponent. It was a matter of the mind, not just the strength of the body, and Essen liked the teachings. He liked it very much.

Then, on a particular evening when the old man was feeling melancholy, he sat down near the fire, folded his arms and began to tell stories, "Have ye heard of the land of the Larmonts?"

"Nay." Essen spread his blanket on the ground, stretched out and turned on his side facing Moran. He sat the puppy beside him, stroked Blue's fur and rested his head on his other arm.

"'Tis in the far north where word has it, the Vikings first landed in Scotland. 'Tis true, right enough, as one of their long ships lay sunken just beyond the shore. Laird Larmont lives in a fine castle atop a hill, that is, if he yet lives. Has been many years since I was there."

"Do the Larmonts have the golden Sword, then?"

"Nay, laddie, the golden sword is in the south of Scotland."

"Is it buried?"

"I do not rightly know. Perhaps so. Were I to have it, I would hide it and burying is the best way. Most believe it is just a legend, but as I have said, my father saw it. The handle is ordinary, but the whole blade is gold and glistens in the sunlight when held up. There is more telling to be done, but we best save it for later. First, you must hear about the land of Essen."

"Essen? The same name as me?"

Moran could not help but smile. "'Tis the best of all names and you are fortunate to have it. Your mother chose wisely. The land of Essen is not a real place, least wise I never believed it was. 'Tis a place a Larmont storyteller often spoke of to delight the children and the elders. I suspect the storyteller has passed by now too." Moran bowed his head for a moment.

"Did the storyteller say of the golden sword?"

Again, the old man smiled. "You are eager to hear, so I will tell you that story first. My father was a good lad, who often traveled the whole of Scotland so he could report his findings to Laird Larmont. Being as the clan was so far north, news of the other clans, and especially what the English were up to, came to us slowly if at all. So Laird Larmont sent two men to seek the news."

The pain in the old man's stomach seemed to be increasing daily, but he shifted his position a little and ignored it. "It was upon one of these journeys that my father and his friend heard of a great war between two clans in the south. Yet the news was perplexing. Some said the village of a clan that lived inside a wall, was set ablaze and all died. But another rumor claimed they escaped through a hidden tunnel and all were saved.

Not long after my father and his friend heard these stories, they happened upon a giant, another lad, a lass and a small laddie. They reported the conflicting stories of the war to the strangers and to their amazement, the lass was delighted to hear it. In celebration, the giant drew a large, golden sword out of its sheath, held it up high and let it glisten in the sunlight.

At first my father feared he would go blind from looking at it and so distracted was he, he did not carefully listen to the words of the lass. The very next day, the lad he was with clutched his chest and fell dead. Father feared he too would die, for the sight of such a magnificent sword might well have been forbidden. He waited for his death, but when it did not come, he dared to repeat the story and soon, all of Scotland was talking about the giant with the golden sword."

"But in all this time, has no one found it?"

"Not that I have heard and such news would surely spread throughout Scotland quickly," Moran answered.

"Then how am I to find it when others could not?"

"My father kept back exactly where he had seen it, just in case the sword held a curse on him if he told. 'Twas upon his death bed years later that he told me, and me alone, where to find it. Now I tell you."

Essen sat up, crossed his legs and listened intently to the instructions. Then he took a moment to commit them to memory before he asked, "But why did you not seek the sword yourself?"

"I thought of it often to be sure. But a lad's life is filled with many things and I did not need the sword to find my happiness."

"Why not?"

"Laddie, there is but one reason to live—the love of a good lass. And children, if a lad is very fortunate. Family is all we truly have in this life and must be cherished far more than anything made of gold."

CHAPTER II

AND SO IT WAS, THAT the old man taught the boy and the dog to survive in a world filled with men, some vile, some saintly and some of a nature not so easy to discover. Essen often asked how Moran knew his name, but there was an art to avoiding the answer and that too, the old man taught the boy. Each day of the short three months they shared, brought more pain and discomfort to the old man's aching stomach, but it was not until he drew his last breath and whispered his final instruction that Essen recognized the voice.

"Bury me not in my clothing, for when you can fully wear them, you will know 'tis time to take your leave."

Moran was dead, but he left a gift more precious than gold. The whispers Essen heard in the night as a child, were not in his mind after all, and suddenly all things became clear. Just as the time had come to bury his mother, it was now time to bury his father. He gently touched the old man's hair, felt the softness of it and remembered the glow in his mother's eyes when she spoke of his father. Love, she once said, is the reason we live. About that, his parents agreed and there it was finally—his banished father lived in the forest and was never very far away. It was he, not his mother, who gave him the name Essen.

So the boy buried his father and returned to the cabin he shared with his mother. The time for growing remained and there was much still to learn. Blue grew the long, shaggy, black and white hair of his breed, half of which always seemed to be over his eyes. Yet the dog did not seem to mind and eventually, Essen came to understand the hair helped hide the dog in the wilderness, just as his father's white clothing blended in with the white rocks of Northern Scotland.

While he could hunt and grow vegetables to sustain himself. He needed more; more knowledge of the world, more warrior skills and a way to make goods to barter on his journey to find the golden sword. Watch and learn, his father advised and the MacKinnon village was the best place to do it. He hid a good distance away, took particular interest in the movements of the warriors as they practiced, and then hurried home to master their techniques with the wooden sword.

Nevertheless, the condition of his clan disturbed him. His people lived in misery under the command of lairds who were greedy men. Of all the temptations in the world, his father once said, wanting to rule over others was the worst. Essen believed his father was right. Sooner or later, the MacKinnon lairds were forced to fight to keep their position and once killed, the next was sometimes better, but often worse. Gold, jewels, wars and the conquering of women were their passions, and they seemed not to care who survived and who did not.

It did not take long for Essen to learn the greatest error a laird made was to indulge himself and neglect his warrior skills. Weakened by strong drink and his pleasures, a coming battle with a laird for power was predictable, and when Essen believed it was near, he went to the village daily to hide and watch. The fight for the highest position in a clan often involved more than just two men and the killings were brutal. Yet Essen kept his wits about him and concentrated on the errors the losers made.

Blue kept him company and Essen spent his nights sewing rabbit skins together, to fashion a warm winter cloak, adding to the shoulder width and the length as he grew. He was delighted each time he made an adjustment, for it appeared he would one day be as big as his father. When his arms grew longer, he made new wooden swords as well.

His MacKinnon kilt and shirt often became too small and from time to time, he was forced to steal larger ones. The making of cloth was not something the old man had time to teach him, nor did Essen have sheep from which to glean the wool.

Once, when he killed a red deer and had no need of all the meat, Essen took some to a woman he deemed uncommonly thin. She too lived apart from the village, and he thought to leave the meat and watch from a distance. He hung it on a high enough peg, but her hungry dogs began to yelp and jump up trying to reach it.

Suddenly, her door opened and he found himself face to face with her bow and arrow. "I mean you no harm," he quickly said. "I brought meat."

Suspicious, she cautiously stuck her head out the door, glanced at the food, yelled at her dogs to be quiet and slowly lowered her bow. "Why?"

"Because you look…I mean, you are alone and you…"

"Have you been watching me?"

He bowed his head. "I have."

She was impressed with his honesty. "There was a time when the lads brought food for me, but I have gotten old." She motioned for him to take down the meat, and then opened her door so he could come in.

Her darkened cottage held few belongings save a bed, two chairs and a table with one leg shorter than the other three. To compensate, a rock under the short leg helped, but the table still looked wobbly and he hesitated to put the meat on it. Even her hearth was small, he could see only one bowl on her shelf and no flask of wine, yet there were several goblets. When she pulled back the window covering, the light greatly improved the look of the place.

She looked older than her years with graying hair, dull brown eyes, and leathery skin denoting years of hard work and not enough food. "I am Lona. 'Tis not such a comely name but it has served me well. Will you cut the meat for me? My hands become feeble these days."

"Will the table fall?"

"Nay." She watched him carefully place the slab of meat on the table, decide it would not fall and draw his dagger. He seemed unusually stout for his size and a hint of a smile crossed her lips when she noticed his awkwardness. Then she turned to fetch her blackened stone pot. She added water from a pitcher and placed each slice of meat he gave her into the container. When he was finished, she washed the table, hung the pot on a hook and began to choose firewood from the pile near her hearth.

"How old are you, laddie?"

"Not yet fourteen."

"I have not laid eyes on you before, what is your name?"

"I am Essen."

Lona suddenly caught her breath. "Your mother let you come this close to the village alone?"

Her question took him completely by surprise. He thought not to answer, but then, his mother could no longer be harmed. "She passed these two years."

Lona let the wood she gathered fall from her hands and grabbed hold of the back of a chair. Then she slowly moved around it until she could sit down. It took time for her to gather her wits. "I feared as much. What of your father?"

"You know my father?"

"Aye, he is my brother."

Essen took a seat at the table and began to explain how he came to know whom his father was. Having someone to talk to about his grief seemed to ease it somehow, and finding family was even more gratifying. He often studied her face to see if he remembered her. Surely, his mother did not come this far without him. If he knew his aunt before, he didn't remember her.

"Lona, why was my father banished?" he asked.

She brushed her tears away and forced herself to tend the fire. The laddie would be hungry and she had just the right spices to make the venison tasty. "Before your birth we had an evil laird."

"Worse than the ones lately?"

That made her smile. "I see I am not the only one you have been watching. Aye, James MacKinnon was far worse. He enjoyed practicing his skill with the bow and arrow by shooting the dogs and letting them suffer. His wife was rarely seen without an injury and sometimes two. We hated him and your father hated him most of all. James MacKinnon tried to take your mother to his bed, so your father called him out."

"Was father banished for killing him?"

"How I wish that were the reason. Nay, your father lost the battle. He took a sword to the stomach and everyone thought he was dead. You mother begged to take him home so she could wash his body and prepare the burial, but he would not let her until she..."

"She what?" Essen asked.

"'Tis best you do not know about that." Lona took a deep breath and continued, "My brother was not dead. In the night, we carried him to a hidden cottage in the forest. But James MacKinnon discovered we had not buried Moran and guessed he was still alive. MacKinnon was enraged and sought his revenge by spreading the word that your father was caught thieving and banished."

"But why did father not take us to live elsewhere?"

"Because news of banishment quickly spreads and he feared you would die with no home at all. He thought to get well, to force James to retract his banishment and then kill him. But by the time he was well enough, Laird James MacKinnon was dead."

Essen's nagging questions had been answered and he was pleased to know all of it finally. He spent nearly a week with the aunt he never knew he had and came back often. He fixed her table, cut wood, carried water, hunted for more meat she could dry and use for later meals, and planted a small vegetable garden behind her cottage.

He learned how to be a man from his father, but from Lona, he learned the ways of women—especially which women to befriend and which to avoid. They were lessons he would not completely understand until much later.

AT THE AGE OF FIFTEEN, he turned his attention to finding something he could make and use for barter on his journey. His mother's two gold coins would not sustain him long, particularly since he had not mastered the art of bartering. It was for this reason he dared enter the MacKinnon village to examine the wares of others.

For the most part, the sizeable village was unkempt. Older cottages were in need of repair, paths were not cleaned, and scorch marks from a long ago fire made the outside of the stone and wood keep seem foreboding. Nevertheless, in the courtyard in front of the Keep, table after table was filled with old and new wares including tools, weapons, fruits, vegetables and breads.

He was virtually a stranger, but of the dozens of people doing their bartering, none seemed to unduly notice him. Few smiled, most contested the outrageously high prices and children kept well away, playing in a meadow instead. The first table held weapons, which he carefully examined and then asked the price. The price quickly disparaged him and soon he moved on to a table filled with tempting delights, most of which he did not recognize. It was then he noticed a man standing on the opposite side of that table watching him. The stranger wore the full dress of a well-trained warrior, and it was plain to see if he didn't do something, Essen was about to be inducted into the service of Laird MacKinnon. Watching without actually looking at the stranger, Essen turned his left foot dramatically inward and hobbled to the next table. It was enough and when he dared glance back, the warrior was gone.

The next table held leather goods where he spotted a well-crafted medallion, picked it up and carefully examined it. He smiled. It was indeed the kind of thing he could make and he already had ample deer hides saved up. Remembering to keep his foot clubbed, he started for home.

It was then he spotted it. In a meadow not far away, a magnificent white colt leaned down to taste the next morsel of grass, and on its forehead, a jagged black mark reminded Essen of a bolt of lightning. Every man needed a horse and this one was young enough to train. To his delight, he had to barter only one of his mother's gold coins and the farmer was so glad to get the price, he threw in a free halter.

Now, there was more than enough to do to keep the young man occupied and the months passed quickly. He made leather medallions and decorated them with small, colorful stones he found in the riverbed and polished. Daily, he practiced his warrior skills, trained Blue and his horse to obey both his verbal and hand commands. Essen named the horse, 'Light,' thinking the word would be easiest to use in a sentence. He hunted, fished, grew vegetables and when he could, he took food to his aunt.

THEY FIT PERFECTLY. At last, Essen put on his father's white shirt, leather belt, kilt and weapons. The boy had become a man, his time was set and on the new moon of the fourth month when he reached his eighteenth year, he gathered his belongings, mounted his horse and with Blue following, set out to find his happiness.

IN NORTHERN SCOTLAND, the King of Scots took up residence in a castle, set high on a hill for protection from his enemies, which he guessed were many. The enormous three-story structure was built of flat stones, one placed atop another and held together by the usual kind of mortar composed of water, sand and lime. Windows were small, but the rooms were plentiful and four guard towers, two on each end of the castle, afforded sufficient views of the land so they could be forewarned of an attack.

Less than three miles away, a short distance on a fast horse, the king's warriors were encamped. By day, they went on guard patrols to scour the land for danger, and at night, their campfires lit up the land all the way around the castle. A large village nearby thrived by making goods with which to supply the king and his men. There was plenty of work to be had and the people were glad to have it, although none was happy to haul their wares up the hill to the castle.

Save for those in the guard towers, window glass had been imported from London to help keep out the cold. Yet, the impurities in the glass made a clear view of the outside nearly impossible, especially when the sun shone on them just so. It was intentional, the King of Scots suspected—the King of England no doubt chose the imperfect glass himself. Therefore, the Scottish king and the other inhabitants of the castle often went to the five-story guard towers, where ample open-air windows on each level, let them enjoy the beauty of the rolling hills, the village and the farmlands.

As the home of any king should be, the rooms were lavishly decorated with an abundance of colorful tapestries on the walls—some of former kings, great battle depictions or magnificent animals. Ornate iron candleholders were evenly spaced, and held candles made of bees wax giving off a sweet smell. Constantly aware of fire danger, servants regularly checked and replaced the candles as necessary. The furniture was well polished, the stone floors swept, the carpets cleaned, the hearths tended to keep away the chill, and the occupants were always well fed.

The king was a tall man with soft brown eyes, light blond hair graying at the temples and a beard and mustache slightly darker than his hair. He was a bit overweight, but it was not his fault. He was often tempted with delights by one servant or another wishing his favors. However, he was not a stupid man, had a vast network of informants and nearly always knew what they were up to even before they did. Seated in his larger than necessary chair at the end of his enormous and splendidly decorated great hall, he usually did not bother putting on his moderately jeweled crown or long red cloak. That practice he reserved for journeys, dinner guests or other special occasions.

Yet he often sat in his particular chair just to remind others who they were dealing with. Not that they could forget in such grand surroundings, with guards posted close enough to protect him, and servants checking the many golden candles holders or offering delights on silver trays.

His days were filled with his commanders, messengers from all over the land and those who wished to make requests of him. Each time he was offered a treat, he tasted the sweet tart or salted meat, gave his praise and waited to see what the servers, all women, would ask. Some requests he granted and others not. Never did he provide an explanation in either case. He was, after all, the King of Scots and not obliged to explain.

Nevertheless, there was one woman's desire he could not discover. Each Tuesday she offered his favorite, took her leave and never asked for a thing. Bethal was as shy as a red fox, he suspected, and as pleasing as the most beautiful of women. The queen was most fond of her and when she pointed out Bethal's excellent skill in the game of Slype-Groat, he was eager to witness it.

The opportunity presented itself one spring evening when the hours of the day were growing longer. With the king seated at one end and the queen at the other, his guests sat along the sides of the long table in the center of the Great Hall, with platters of tempting delights and chalices of wine spread out before them. When the meal was finished, the king left his chair and motioned for the servers to clear his end of the table. He removed his crown, shed his cloak, handed them off to a waiting boy, straightened his kilt and challenged Bethal to do her best.

Seated beside the queen at the opposite end of the table, Bethal grinned, stood up and curtsied. "And if I win, will you have me done in, my king?" She wore the red and black colors of her king proudly with a red long shirt beneath her ankle length, belted plaid. Her leather shoes were soft and comfortable, and her deep red hair was fashioned in the usual long, loose braid down the middle of her back. Yet her most glowing feature was her green eyes, which mesmerized the king as much as any man at first sight of her.

He raised an eyebrow and ignored the giggles of the ladies. "You will not win. I am most proficient at this game and rarely lose."

Bethal walked to a small table near the wall, picked up the king's four-hands by eight-hands Slype-Groat board and carried it to the long table. "Aye, but I will not let you win as others may." Still holding it, Bethal gently ran her fingers over the smooth surface of the board.

The king had been mistaken—Bethal was not shy at all and instead, had the tenacity and the courage to banter with him, which he found captivating. "Let me win? I think not. Tell me, does my board meet with your approval?"

Bethal laid the board on the table. Then she took a step back, leaned down until her eyes were level with the board and searched for slight bulges or dips in the polished wood. Many had such boards in Scotland, but they were not easily made. The diagonal and vertical grooves in the wood had to measure exactly the same, rendering the squares just a little larger than the coin. "It will do, I suppose."

The king looked at the queen and rolled his eyes. "I suppose you wish to inspect my coins as well. Have a look, Bethal, you will find an assortment in a bowl on the same table where you found the board. By the way, how did you know where to find the board? Have you been skulking around in my absence?"

"Indeed not. I have heard you have the finest board in all of Scotland and I spotted it once when I served you. I longed to touch it and now you have graciously allowed it. You are a very good king."

Both his eyebrows shot up. "Flattery? Do you flatter me to throw me off my game?"

A slow grin crossed her face. "Will it work, do you think?" Amid roars of laughter, she walked to the small table to examine the coins. Choosing three, she made sure they were smooth on both sides and then carried the small bowl to him. "Does the king wish me to choose coins for him?"

"I believe I best choose my own. You may try to trick me."

"Trickery, I learned from my laird, renders the game quite unworthy."

"And who is your laird?"

"Justin MacGreagor."

"Ah yes, I remember now." The king chose three, tossed them back and chose three other coins. Satisfied, he set the bowl on the table. "Tell me, is Justin a stern lad?"

"Not at all, save when a lass or a wee one is in danger. He is very protective of us and hardly lets us out of his sight. However, he can be persuaded occasionally, as you see. She grinned and half curtsied."

"And how does he keep the village so clean? Never have I been to a village in Scotland so well kept."

She toyed with the coins in her hand for a moment. "'Tis a secret, but I suppose 'twill not hurt to tell you. When a parent has had enough of a child's bad behavior, he or she is sent to Justin and must confess the crime. Justin glares at the child for a time and then gives over a punishment, which is always some sort of cleaning. The worst crime is thievery, for which the guilty must clean the horse droppings for as long as a fortnight."

The king wrinkled his brow, turned up his nose at the thought and then began to chuckle. "Very good, very good indeed." He too bent down to examine the board for irregularities. A particularly humid day could sometimes warp the wood ever so slightly. "Each year lairds send me an unmarried lass to learn the ways of the queen's court. Most are spies. What have you to say to that?"

"I say give me their names and I will call them out. I am most accomplished with a bow and arrow, providing my opponent is not more than six or I dare say seven years of age."

Bethal grinned, laid her coins on the bottom of the board with an edge of each slightly protruding over the end. "With your permission." She didn't wait for an answer before she struck the overhanging edge of the coins with the palm of her hand and sent them sliding toward the top.

Instantly the king leaned closer to see just how many rested in the middle of the squares without touching any of the grooves. "Ah ha, I challenge this one," he said.

She too took time to scrutinize the position of the coins. "As you wish, but I claim two points for the others."

He stroked his beard for a moment, closely examined the other two and at length nodded. "Two points it is. Shall we have the queen keep our score? Perhaps not, she greatly favors you."

"Aye, but she *loves* you."

He turned to see the glow in his wife's eyes and winked at her. A comely woman in her own right, the queen wore her golden hair in the two braids he preferred and returned his smile. "Has she told you this?"

"Quite often I am afraid. It becomes tedious at times."

The king turned his attention back to the game. "Tedious? How so?"

Bethal watched him carefully line up his coins. "I quite envy her, you see. I too wish to be in love."

"I see. Would you like my assistance? I believe I can arrange a marriage to any lad you wish, even a married one. It might take a bit longer, but it can be arranged."

Bethal bowed her head. "You are as good to me as any father could be, my king, but I wish to make my own way in the world."

He was taken aback by being called fatherly, but he let it pass. There would be time enough to contemplate his image later. Instead, he changed the position of each of his coins on the board. "Bethal, you came to serve me in October, and this is the month of April. Have you seen no lad in my court that stirs your fancy?"

"When I am not serving you, my king, I tend your children and when not that, your wife desires me to..."

"I see. In that case, you are exposed to no other men save the groomsmen, the gardeners, my guards and a hand full of servants. If memory serves me correctly, they already have wives."

"Precisely."

The king looked perplexed for a moment and then he grinned. "I see I have been outwitted. You make no request when you serve me, but just now, you say it in such a round-about way, I am inclined to grant it. Are you wanting to go home, Bethal?"

"I confess, I am. I shall greatly miss my queen, but I hope for a MacGreagor husband."

He leaned a little closer to her, yet spoke loud enough for all to here. "If you let me win, I shall grant it immediately."

Bethal pretended to be shocked and then narrowed her eyes. "Let you win? Disgrace myself? I do not wish to go home that badly."

At that moment, Bethal, daughter of Bethia and Hannish MacGreagor, won a place in the heart of the King of Scots. Never again was her desire to leave brought up and for days, they played the game, when his duties did not demand his attention elsewhere. More often than not he lost, which only served to sharpen his desire to win. He had not forgotten her request and hoped she would willingly stay after her time was up, but occasionally, he would find Bethal staring aimlessly out a window and knew she longed to be with her family.

There could be only one answer—he would find her a husband who would live nearby and let her remain in his company. Then he would let her see the MacGreagors twice a year so she would not miss them so much. To that end, he invited various men to spend an evening with him and made certain Bethal was put upon to attend. Several lads were quickly smitten, but she found none of them pleasing. She wanted a MacGreagor husband and would have no other. He thought to force a marriage, but then, he happened upon a more intriguing idea.

CHAPTER III

IT WAS NOT AS IF HE were watching her from a hiding place. Instead, Essen stood next to his horse in full view of a woman who did not give him the slightest notice. For days he made his way south through the forest until he came to a creek and then followed it downhill as his father instructed. To find the sword, he must first find the people, and perhaps this creek would lead him to the place where the sword was last seen. Along the way, he happened upon a cottage and decided to ask directions.

Her cottage was old, the land around it had not been worked in years and he wondered how the woman managed to survive. It appeared she was all alone. She looked to be in her forties, her graying hair was uncombed, her cheeks were a brighter red than normal, and although her clothing was not overly dirty, they were faded and beginning to fray. He might have discovered the color of her eyes had she once looked at him, but she did not. Blue whimpered, but one frown from Essen made the dog sit and be quiet.

"I hate every bit of you," the woman muttered. She walked right past Essen, entered her cottage, came back out, spread a deer hide over a low tree branch and began to beat it with a stick. At first, a cloud of dust filled the air, but long after the dust dissipated she was still beating the pelt. "You'll not darken my door again. You are evil and I'll not let you stay no matter the promise. You ate all I had and walked away without giving my reward. And you, my own brother. You burned me, aye, you did. I..."

The volume of her ranting increased, as did the severity with which she beat the skin, and several times Essen looked around trying to see where her brother might be hiding. As near as he could tell, he was the only other person there. It might not have been so unusual had she acknowledged him. After all, Essen sometimes talked to himself as well. Still, not noticing a man standing right in front of her was odd, very odd indeed.

He feared he might startle her, but he asked it anyway, "I seek the golden sword. Do you know where it is?"

"No one knows where it is," she answered without turning his direction or interrupting the rhythm of her hide beating. "I heard tell the King of Scots has it. Then I heard tell the lass put a curse on it and they that touch it fall dead away. 'Twas a little laddie with the lass, but none know what's become of him."

Essen marveled that she could so easily speak and keep right on beating the hide. "I will not harm you."

"Nay, you will not. My lads will protect me."

"What lads?"

"They be right behind you."

Alarmed, he quickly drew his sword and spun around, but he could see no one in any direction. It took a moment to calm himself before he thought to ask, "Who is behind me?"

"The dead."

He wrinkled his brow and slowly began to put his sword away. "Is it to the dead you speak?"

The woman frowned. "Who else is here? Be gone with you, you be tiresome."

It took but a moment to comply with her wishes. Blue was even happier to be leaving and raced on ahead. She was the first truly daft person of Essen's acquaintance, and he wondered if there were many more, who spoke to and were able to see the dead. He hoped not, but just in case, he charged himself to be far more cautious when approaching a lone cottage in the future.

PATCHES MACGREAGOR had several things on her mind and taking a husband was not one of them. The youngest of Laird Justin MacGreagor's four sisters, she longed for adventure—any sort of adventure. Life was pleasant, but often boring enough to make most everyone miserable. If only she had been born a man, she would have gladly become a hunter or a guard so she could meet strangers on the paths, hear the gossip first hand and see much more of the world.

She lived in a well-kept village near a river at the end of a long, wide glen. There were ample trees, fresh water, good hunting and plenty of pasture for the livestock. Wild flowers grew in abundance, birds chirped in the trees and occasionally, a golden eagle soared through the air from one end of the glen to the other.

The Keep, where she shared the second floor with her aging mother, was the center of the clan's existence. The great hall on the bottom floor was large enough to hold a hundred people if need be, and it was usually occupied by her brother Justin's advisors and countless men, constantly coming in with questions or awaiting orders.

All the rooms were decorated with wall tapestries, although some were well worn, especially the large one of a red deer in the great hall. Yet the family could not seem to part with it. Another wall in the great hall held a display of weapons, both old and new. Large stuffed pillows along the walls added color and comfort when some were required to sit on the floor. The rest of the room was not unlike many other keeps, with a long table and tall back chairs in the center, a large stone hearth in the far corner, a door in the back to a kitchen and an enclosed staircase leading to the upper bedchambers. Laird Justin MacGreagor shared the third floor bedchamber with his wife, Deora, and their two toddler daughters.

Directly in front of the Keep was a wide courtyard with a hip-high stonewall along the outer edge. The wall was where the people often sat to watch the children play, or more importantly to watch in the evenings, to see which man would approach which woman during the customary time for courting. It was a favorite pastime, almost as beloved as gossiping and there was plenty to be had of that.

Gossip brought the news and even when clans were at war, the network of guards could set aside their differences, and get word of an English attack to the king in the north in as little as two days. Indeed, gossip never stopped and the people counted on the guards providing it each evening when they returned. It was yet another reason to gather in the courtyard.

As was the MacGreagor custom, the village was kept in good repair, the paths between the cottages were often swept and the people themselves bathed almost daily, depending on the weather and their health. A recently added stable not far from the courtyard held only three horses—the laird's and those belonging to his second and third in command. Beside it was a storehouse where wood for hearths was kept dry, especially during winter.

Patches loved her family and the whole clan loved her, save perhaps Brevie. Her propensity to tear her clothing often when she was small earned her the nickname, Patches, and she'd been called that for so long, she doubted anyone knew her Christian name. It mattered not, since strangers came only to see her brother and she was never introduced and not old enough to be presented - a custom reserved for times when a laird wanted to marry a woman off.

It was of seeing a vast English manor or perhaps a Scottish castle she was thinking, when she fell into line behind a group of women and children headed to the loch to bathe. The women enjoyed the solitude of the tree and rock lined loch in the morning, while the men bathed after their labors in the evening. As they always did on their arrival, the women spread out around the edge of the water and began to disrobe.

Most often Patches paid no particular attention to who was near, but when she discovered Brevie walking beside her on the path, she frowned. The ongoing disagreement with Brevie, a young woman her same age, started long ago and for no specific reason Patches was aware of.

It seemed they were the only two that did not get along. Everyone else in their age group thought Brevie was bright and cheerful, loved her laughter and sought her out when they wanted advice. Patches normally managed to avoid her, but not this morning and even when she walked around the loch to the far end of the other women, Brevie followed.

As soon as Patches gave up, stopped and began to undress, Brevie removed her belt, her white shirt and her predominantly green plaid, with light blue squares that matched the skirts of all the other women. Brevie folded her clothing, laid them on a rock and followed Patches into the water. "I wish to have a word with you."

"What about?"

"'Tis time you take a husband and the sooner the better."

Patches rolled her eyes. Completely disinterested in the discussion, she submerged in the cool water to wet her long, light brown hair. Like her mother, Glenna, and her oldest sister, Ceanna, it was wavy enough to curl around her face when it was dry and she preferred to wear it loose when it was not too hot or humid—which was not often considering Scotland's unpredictable climate.

Brevie did not mind waiting to have her say. Everyone, even Patches, had to come up for air sometime. While she waited, she finished unbraiding her dark hair. At last, her rival's head broke the surface of the water. "It is unfair for you to remain unmarried."

"Unfair to whom?"

"To me for one." She quickly put her head under the surface of the water and then, beginning with her arms, Brevie meticulously began to rub soap on her body.

Not nearly so particular, Patches quickly added soap to her wet hair and then the rest of her body. "'Tis the first I've heard this complaint. How could it possibly be unfair to you?"

"I have said it before and I will say it again. You are addle brained, Patches MacGreagor. You cannot see what is before your very eyes."

"And I suppose you have been appointed to enlighten me. Carry on then, I cannot wait." Instead of waiting, Patches submerged again to rinse the soap out of her hair.

Brevie rolled her eyes, finished soaping her hair and then submerged as well. Knowing Patches, the girl would stay down as long as possible to avoid the answer, and Brevie decided she might as well use the time to her own advantage. Finally, both heads were out of the water. "Your brother has no sons," Brevie blurted out soon after she filled her lungs with air.

"What could that possibly matter?" Intrigued suddenly, she followed Brevie out of the water, grabbed the faded cloth she brought with her and began to dry off.

Just as meticulously as she washed, Brevie started with her hair and then used her cloth to dry the rest of her body. The air was unusually warm and she would have liked lingering in the water longer. Unfortunately, there were chores that needed to be done and this was the perfect opportunity to talk to Patches.

Patches already had her shirt and belt on and was beginning to pleat her plaid. "So what if my brother has no sons?"

"You amaze me. I did not think anyone was that simple. Who will become the next laird if Justin has no sons?"

"Justin will not choose the next laird, the people will. Everyone knows that."

"Therein lies the problem. Justin surrounds himself with family, namely the men married to his sisters. He appointed two of them to high positions and when he dies, the people will quite naturally turn to the ones Justin trusted most."

Patches narrowed her soft blue eyes. "Hold your tongue, Brevie MacGreagor. Justin will not die, not anytime soon at least, and choosing a new laird will not happen for years to come."

"People die of all kinds of unhappiness and never when we expect it."

"I do not wish to talk of this." Remembering where they were suddenly, she looked around. All the other women were nearly finished bathing, most were dressed and on their way back to the village.

Brevie abruptly grabbed Patches' arm. "Listen and listen well. Lads hope to become your husband, so they may be part of Justin's family and hold a high position. Do you not see? The husband of Patches MacGreagor will have a better chance of becoming laird? There are some who will do anything to gain that advantage."

"Even marry me?"

"Especially marry you."

Patches slowly closed her eyes, thought about it and then opened them again. "You may let go of me now."

Brevie forgot about her firm grip and quickly withdrew her hand. Suddenly her demeanor completely changed. "Have I hurt you? I did not mean to."

"A little perhaps, but not badly. Brevie, you are still half-naked. You might pay a little more attention to dressing." Patches sat down on a rock and began to put on her shoes. "Tell me, do others say the same?"

"Are you going to tell your brother I hurt you?"

Patches was surprised by the question and forgot her shoes in favor of studying the look of terror in the other woman's eyes. They were clearly not friends, but the thought that Brevie feared her, never once entered her mind. It was true; there was an edict proclaiming death to a man who intentionally hurt a woman or a child. It was a necessary edict considering MacGreagor men were very large and kept themselves strong. Yet she had never once heard of it being applied to a woman. Of course, it could be, she supposed, but banishment was the only punishment for a woman she had ever heard of. Even then, the MacGreagors would see that the woman was taken safely to the clan of her choice.

Brevie's fear of her changed everything. Never before had she considered who she actually was and what being Laird Justin MacGreagor's sister meant. Perhaps she was simple minded after all. Her voice was much softer when she spoke this time, "We are not friends, you and I, but I know you did not mean to hurt me. We will say no more of it. Now tell me, do all the lasses resent my not taking a husband?"

Relieved, Brevie finished pleating her skirt and sat down on a nearby rock to put on her shoes. "I am not privy to how all of them feel, but some do."

"Then they should just tell me which lads they favor and I will find a way of discouraging them."

Brevie clicked her tongue on the top of her mouth. "Still you do not see. Tell your brother you are ready to take a husband, let the lads approach you and let the rest of us see which they are."

Her irritation quickly returned and Patches began to raise her voice. "You allow that no lad could truly want me for myself alone?"

"Perhaps one or two might, but there are others who are dishonorable—possibly."

"I see, marrying me off to a dishonorable lad would make you and the other lasses happy."

"You need not marry one of them, but you must see the advantage to the rest of us."

Patches looked away. Something more was going on here. "Is there a particular lad you are unsure of? Has he said or done something that makes you suspect him?" She waited but Brevie only bit her lip and did not answer. "I see. And if he does approach, would you let me marry him?" Again there was no answer. "It is plain you hate me, but I never imagined you would wish such misery on me."

"I do not hate you, but I do not forgive you either."

"Forgive me for what? What have I done?"

Brevie stood up and mockingly curtsied. "I might have known you would not remember. Never mind all that now, my only concern is to marry a lad who does not want *you*!" With that, she turned and walked away.

Patches remained on the rock with one shoe on and the other in her lap trying to understand. The truth was, she was part of a family highly regarded and honored by the rest of the clan, by virtue of her brother's position. Her father and his father before him had also been MacGreagor lairds and were greatly loved by the clan. She didn't often play with the other children, but it was not because she was forbidden. It was because she had three older sisters and an older brother to entertain her.

When she was old enough, she was taught how to fight with the other young women. Yet, it was hardly a social gathering and now that she thought about it, she had no friends closer than any others. Perhaps having a close friend or two might have kept her from hearing the truth from someone who hated her, if indeed it was the truth. Hearing it from Brevie was utterly humiliating.

Patches bowed her head and tried to think. Had any of the men paid undue attention to her lately? Donan smiled at her once, but that was no indication he preferred her. Other men smiled at her sometimes too—even married men. As hard as she might, she could not discover who Brevie thought would approach her. It occurred to her Justin would know what a man was up to and forbid such a marriage. But then, what if Justin did not discern it correctly? He was, after all, occasionally wrong.

Patches considered the husbands of her sisters. Shaw married Brenna, but he was already Justin's second in command at the time. The oldest sister, Ceanna, married Ginnion and he too was already one of Justin's favorites. Carley did not marry until a year ago and Patches had to admit she liked Mefrin the least. Mefrin did nothing wrong particularly, he was just never as attentive to Carley as the husbands of the other sisters. It did not mean he did not love her; he was simply not the affectionate kind.

What could be done to discover the truth of a man's intentions? She could, Patches thought, tell Justin she was ready to marry and then reject every man who approached her. She dismissed that idea almost immediately. A woman could run out of prospective husbands far too quickly that way and when she was truly ready, she might be left with just a soppy laddie and a very old lad to choose from.

Patches sighed, put on her other shoe and headed up the path to the village.

ESSEN HAD NO REAL IDEA what to expect when he set out to find the sword, but the land was far more vast than he imagined, with as much as a day's ride between some of the villages. There appeared to be enough room in Scotland to house all the people in the world. Some clans preferred to live out in the open, and he could see the advantages of not letting warring clans attack from hiding places in the trees. However, those villages were difficult to observe from afar. Lying down on the tops of hills helped, but he sometimes found himself crawling from rock to rock, hoping his white clothing would keep him from being seen.

Only the people in one village made him turn away and continue on. That clan was obviously preparing for war and the appointed time was not far off. Men were sharpening swords, making more arrows and testing the strength of the strings on their crossbows. Horses were being prepared and they were not the slower horses better suited for long distances, but the sleeker, faster breeds. He thought to wait just to see which direction they would ride, but decided to make a swift retreat back to the forest instead.

Clans often went to war over land, his father said, but there was so much land, Essen could see no reason to fight over it. Once back in the forest and well hidden, he decided to let his horse rest for the remainder of the day. Yet the forest seemed far more quiet than usual. Not long after, he heard the thunder of horse's hooves. For a moment, he believed the hordes of men were headed straight for him, but the noise began to dissipate and Essen breathed a sigh of relief.

WHEN HE APPROACHED the next small village, Essen was even more wary and halted to watch for a time. He needed supplies and hoped this was the best place to barter for them. It seemed to be an ordinary village with some thirty or so cottages surrounding a larger stone building. It looked much like that of the MacKinnon Clan except it was considerably smaller. The people were ordinary, he could see no men fighting and some in the clan actually smiled—which was most uncommon in the MacKinnon village.

He would not stay long, he decided as he urged his horse onto the path and started for the courtyard. To his surprise, as soon as he got down off his horse, he was greeted by two women instead of armed men. Both women moved closer and favored him with a shy sort of smile. He quickly glanced around and still no men came to ask his business or to protect the women.

"I am Vinna," the first said. "She is Epona. We are unmarried." Vinna covered her mouth and joined her sister in a giggle. "Are you married?"

He wasn't certain he should answer that and he could feel Epona's hand stroking the back of his. It unnerved him and he took a step back.

These were the kind of women his aunt warned him about, he guessed. "I wish to barter for goods and that is all."

Vinna pouted. "Perhaps you are not lad enough to make a wife happy."

Essen remembered to be pleasant but firm as his aunt advised. "You are both tempting, but I have no need of a wife." He curtly bowed, walked around them and pulled away from their tugs on his arm. Even so, he could feel them follow him across the courtyard where only two tables were filled with wares to barter. He examined the goods on the first table, found nothing he wanted and moved on.

The second table held vegetables, fish that did not smell too fresh and open bags of ginger, pepper and saffron. Larger bags offered beans, carrots, turnips, oats, and barley. Essen reached into his shirt, pulled out a medallion, lifted the thin leather strap over his head, and handed it to the woman seated on the other side of the table. She examined it, smiled and when she nodded, he opened his sack, chose a handful of turnips, several carrots, two onions, and a loaf of bread. Then he closed the sack, tied it around his waist and opened a smaller one, which he filled with barley.

"Have you no lads in this clan?" he asked as he closed and tied the second sack around his waist.

"Aye, but they are few. My sisters need husbands, are you willing?"

The mention of marriage twice in such a short period of time unsettled him and when he looked, Vinna and Epona wore determined expressions, and both had their daggers drawn. "Light Blue," he shouted. At Essen's side, Blue showed his sharp teeth and viciously growled at the women, forcing them to move back. At the same time, Light raced to pick up his rider. Essen put both hands on the back of his moving horse, swung a leg over, grabbed a hand full of mane just before Light jumped a hedge and sped off.

It was not until he felt himself safely away that he stopped. He built a small fire, began to grind the barley in a bowl and mix it with yeast, to make hot cakes. Some women were not forthcoming, his aunt warned, but he had not thought them truly dangerous until now. Where were all the men? Surely they had a laird at least. He had no answer and he certainly did not intend to go back, no matter how curious he was.

His stomach full finally, he made his bed, stretched out, covered himself and let Blue lay down beside him.

CHAPTER IV

THE NEXT DAY, PATCHES tried desperately to concentrate on her sewing, but Brevie's words haunted her and she needed someone to talk to about it. If it was true, surely there were others who suspected men hoped to marry her for all the wrong reasons. She put down her work, left her bedchamber, walked down the stairs and made her way through the normal host of men in the great hall, all trying to talk to her brother at the same time.

She smiled when she realized what they were talking about. As they had a million times before, and as a result of unresolved boredom, they were debating the pros and cons of building a wall around the village. Half feared being trapped inside, while the other half believed a wall would keep the children safe from wild boars, and the chickens safe from red foxes. There never seemed to be a clear majority on either side.

At last, she was outside. Patches paused for a moment to decide which way to go. The air was warm and the ground not muddy for a change, so she chose the path that led all the way down the middle of the glen. On the backside of the village, a river that occasionally flooded its banks, offered plenty of fresh water and fishing, but the paths next to the river soon took one out of sight of the guards. The women in particular were not encouraged to walk those paths, unless a man accompanied them for protection. There did not seem to be currently, but in the past a shortage of women tempted men from other clans to snatch one. It not only put the woman in danger, but it often led to a brutal and deadly clan war.

Each year new cottages were added as the clan grew and when the elders passed or a plague crossed the land, empty cottages were given to the newly married, to the oldest in families with too many children or saved for sojourners. Never were the cottages built in straight rows, therefore the paths meandered at odd angles between them. The path down the middle of the glen was the only straight one and it was in the glen that most took their morning or evening walks.

Not far from the edge of the village, a section of land was reserved for the daily warrior training. Beyond that were the corrals used to keep the stallions from fighting over the mares in heat. Behind it, the forest was thick and held raspberry bushes that would soon yield their fruit. A delight everyone was impatiently waiting for.

On the other side of the path, were mares and cattle nibbling on grass and wild flowers, while sheep grazed in the adjoining valleys. In the spring, nearly everyone came to watch the new colts or calves and therefore, several rows of logs lined that side of the glen. With the days growing longer, it was not unusual for whole families to enjoy their evening meal there.

Beyond the logs, the MacGreagor graveyard held loved ones who had been carefully laid to rest in strong wooden boxes. Their names were sometimes carved in tall, flat rocks that stood upright at the head of the graves.

Patches considered visiting her father's resting place. It always seemed to comfort her, but this time she needed answers more than comfort. She was so engrossed in her thoughts; she hardly noticed groups of women standing around talking or children playing in the glen.

She loved Justin's wife, Deora, who always gave good advice, but Mistress Deora had her hands full with two young daughters, the cleaning supervision of a three-story keep and the selection of the food they would eat. More often than not, the entire family gathered for an evening meal—all fourteen of them.

Once married, her sisters moved into cottages with their husbands. Both Ceanna, the eldest and Brenna, the second had their own children to care for, but with such loving husbands as their's, Patches was certain both would dismiss her worries as foolish and perhaps even laugh at her.

Growing up the youngest of five with only one brother to protect her, she often had more advisors than any one little girl could ever need. Carley, the one closest to her in age, was the least bothersome. As Patches got older, she discovered Carley was the wisest and nearly always the best one to ask. However, Carley did not seem content lately. Their mother suspected another grandchild on the way, but no happy announcement had been made.

Before she realized it, Patches had already walked half way down the glen. Not as fond of animals as others were, she nevertheless found herself at the fence of the spacious corral watching a man shoe a horse. A few minutes later, she spotted Donan standing in the forest watching her. She smiled and when she did, he came to her and took up a position not far from her at the fence.

"May I ask you a question?"

Donan was a tall man with the broad shoulders of a warrior, who took keeping in good physical shape seriously. When the men finished warrior training and then ran the length of the glen and back, Donan often took an extra run up one of the rolling hills and down again. He liked running and often won races at feasts or festivals. "What is your question?"

"Do you think a lad will want to marry me just to improve his chances of becoming laird?"

He did not quickly answer. Years before, the MacGreagor and MacClurg clans joined together, and now they numbered nearly a thousand. He was not often around Justin and his family, couldn't remember ever having a discussion with Patches and was not prepared for her directness. "Has a lad approached you?"

"Nay, I am not yet ready to marry. But when I am, should I fret over a lad's intentions?"

"Well, let me see. A laird makes all the rules, lives in a fine keep, controls the wealth and is obeyed by all. I suppose there are some men who desire such power."

"Do you?"

"Would I admit it, if I did?"

She realized her error and smiled. "'Tis not a question I can simply ask the lad who approaches me, is it?"

It was the first time he'd seen the dimples in her cheeks up close and he found them very pleasing. "Nay."

"What can I do, then?"

"I do not know. It is often impossible to discern a lad's motives or that of a lass either. There are many lasses who would marry a laird simply to become mistress over his clan."

"Then I pity the lairds."

That made him smile. He turned around, leaned against the fence and folded his arms. "As do I. I have heard marriage to an unhappy lass can do a lad in."

"Aye, but lads can set an unwanted wife aside."

"True, but he must petition the Pope and who knows how long that can take. A lad might easily die before he is free of her."

Patches had known who Donan was all her life, but it was the first time she realized how big he was. She was tall yet she was forced to look up to see his facial expressions. "But can a lad not leave a wife and join another clan?"

"That too is not easily done. If a lad came to us and asked to be in our clan, what would you suspect him of?"

The answer came quickly. "Of being banished from his own clan for unspeakable crimes."

"Precisely. We are born into a clan and stay until we are buried, like it or not."

She wrinkled her brow. "Do you wish to leave the MacGreagors?"

"Not at all. I am happy here and from what I have heard of other clans, this is paradise. Your brother keeps us out of war, our lasses are becoming and the children good humored. What more could a lad want?"

"Well I want for adventure. There is not enough to do, we see few strangers and often hear of excitement and trickery elsewhere." At the sound of a far off whistle, Patches turned around. "Perhaps my excitement is coming now." She flashed her grin at him and headed home.

It was early afternoon when the whistles began at the mouth of the long MacGreagor glen. After that, the whistle was repeated by other men until the announcement of approaching strangers reached the village and the Keep. The curious quickly began to fill the courtyard or step out of their cottages onto the paths to watch. By the time the riders drew near, there was no question as to their identity. They wore the red shirt, red and black kilt and the red cloak of the King of Scots. Even their shields displayed the King's crown and they rode atop red plaids over the backs of their mounts.

It was an impressive display and everyone hoped the King was among them, but it was a hope soon dispelled. The riders numbered only three and surely the King would arrive with a much larger guard. The question on the lips of every man and woman was—do they bring good news or bad? When the faces of the messengers held no hint, they feared the news was bad. And when the visitors reached the courtyard, and the one in the middle announced he wished to speak to Laird Justin MacGreagor alone, they were certain it was very bad news indeed.

The crowd quietly watched as Justin invited the man inside the great hall and closed the door. A large man of six feet, four inches, Laird Justin MacGreagor wore his dark hair shoulder length, his beard well-trimmed and had his grandmother, Anna's, brilliant blue eyes. It was thought he came from Viking ancestors, though no one knew for sure and besides, everyone knew Vikings had blond hair. He kept himself in good physical condition, in case there was a war and when Justin glared, there were few men who cared to oppose him. Fortunately for the clan, he seldom glared and was, for the most part, a gentle man.

Even so, Justin was a reluctant laird. Years before it was decreed that the people would choose their laird rather than see men fight and die for the right. Although his father, his grandfather and his great-grandfather had been MacGreagor lairds, there was a chance he would not be selected. It was not that he didn't love the people, he did, but lairds had little private time to fish, hunt and be with his family. Being with his father more was a thing Justin sorely missed growing up and hoped not to pass to his own son.

Yet when his father passed, the people asked him to be their laird and he agreed, thinking it would be only be for a time. That was years ago and Justin was still waiting for his first son to be born. He cherished his daughters and spent as much time as he could with them, but his attention was always in high demand—so much so, he almost wished Deora would not give him any sons, so the family would be rid of the tradition. He was just on his way up the stairs to spend time with his little family when the whistles began announcing the king's men.

Justin urged the smaller man to take a seat at the table and poured him a goblet of wine. "Welcome Isolt. To what do we owe this great honor? I have seen the King but twice and you only four or five times in the years I have been laird."

The King's messenger gulped down half his wine and then wiped a small spill off his beard with the back of his hand. "The King desires you to bring five unmarried men to him in a fortnight."

Justin took his seat at the head of the table and stared downward for a moment. "Why?"

Isolt's beard and mustache were the same bright red as his hair and he absentmindedly brushed his mustache outward with his thumb and forefinger. "There are rumors to be sure, but the King did not confide in me."

"Unmarried men? What could he possibly be up to? Have you no guess at all?"

"Well, there is another command. Of the five, one will be chosen to remain in the King's service."

"Does he also choose a lad from the other clans?"

"I have no such messages for the other clans."

It was perplexing. Choosing men to be in the king's service was not so very odd, Justin thought, but why only unmarried? Then a thought occurred to him and he smiled. "How is our Bethal?"

Isolt grinned. Justin had come to the same conclusion he had. "I have heard she is the delight of all who meet her. Several of the king's men were brought about to tempt her, but she chose to marry none of them."

"Our Bethal wants a MacGreagor husband. Tell me, is our king in good health?"

"He has the usual plagues on his good health. Two sons have died at birth."

"We heard that. Are there other plagues?"

"Other than rumors of wars and rebellions, I have heard of none. Will you obey his command?"

"I will, if only to see what the king is up to. Stay the night, we offer good beds and a fine meal."

"We cannot, we have other messages to deliver. But we will accept bread and vegetables if you have them to spare. Our supplies run low."

Justin went to the door, motioned for Ginnion to come and told him to see to a hearty bag of food for the king's men to take. An hour later, and after a good meal, Justin gave them the supplies, bid the king's men goodbye, watched them ride up the gradual slope of a hill and disappear over the top.

He was not surprised to find his people still in the courtyard waiting to hear the bad news. He chose his words wisely, "I have been commanded to see the King in a fortnight and I am to bring five unmarried men with me. One will be chosen to remain in the king's service."

It was not such bad news after all, and some in the crowd were openly relieved. Yet a few of the unmarried women were not pleased at all and were not afraid to show it. Justin noticed one woman's glare, turned and walked down the path toward the river.

The large flat rock near the bank of the river was his favorite place to be alone and everyone knew not to bother him there. Still, people could see him and he could not let down his guard or let his face betray his feelings. A sad or even a happy expression would lead the clan to speculate and often the rumors became outrageous.

Justin found himself looking forward to time away. Still, one thing bothered him—if the king wanted a man to marry Bethal and offered a position to keep him there, he meant to keep Bethal as well. Should he share his suspicions with Bethal's parents? She had to beg them to let her go the previous fall and her mother worried about her daily. Not telling them the king wanted to keep her would be unkind. Then again, the king's command might have nothing to do with Bethal and getting them riled over nothing served no purpose. He decided against telling them and turned his attention instead to choosing the best men to take with him.

He had not heard her approach and was surprised to find Patches standing near him. "I wish to be alone."

"I wish to ask a question."

"Now? Can it not wait?"

"Have you any idea how hard it is to find you alone?"

Justin smiled, took her hand and tugged until she sat down beside him. "I have often heard this complaint from my wife." He put his arm around her and hugged his little sister. "What could possibly need my attention?"

"Which lads will you take with you?"

"I was just thinking about that. Have you a desire to see one or more stay behind?"

Patches rolled her eyes. "I care not who you take. If one is chosen by the king, I will have one less to fret over."

He wrinkled his brow. "Fret over? Do you wish to explain?"

She was quiet for a while before she spoke. "Nay, I only wish to ask a question."

"You want my permission to take a husband?"

"Not yet, it is just that—Justin, if I chose the wrong lad to marry, would you prevent it?"

"MacGreagor lasses are allowed to marry whomever they wish. But if I thought it a bad match, I would try to change your mind."

"Good." She stood up, bent down and kissed his cheek. "I am counting on you to keep your word."

Perplexed, he watched her walk away. Patches did not want a husband, but just in case, she wanted his pledge to prevent it if she chose the wrong man? He was beginning to think he understood less and less about women every day. Being short of understanding was not a pleasant position for a laird to find himself in. He made a mental note to talk to his wife about Patches later and turned his attention back to choosing the five men he would take with him.

It was not that easy to decide. Some were very skilled warriors and he needed them. Others had trades essential to the wellbeing of the clan such as building, forging and shoemaking. Moreover, he wanted to choose men who would make good husbands. This decision, he decided, could take a while.

THE SECOND FLOOR OF the Keep held two bedchambers and a sitting room. The sparsely furnished bedchamber Patches slept in was all hers now that her sisters were married. Rarely did anyone disturb her there. Her favorite wall hanging was a drawing of her as a child on parchment. It hung above her bed and she smiled every time she remembered having to sit so ceaselessly still for the artist. Now she loved it and was happy she had.

She hated weapons and would have preferred not having them hung on her wall, but all women had to be able to defend themselves and their children. She obediently wore a dagger tied around her waist, but she kept her sword hanging from a peg on her wall within easy reach. On the other wall, a colorful tapestry once belonging to her grandmother, Anna, brightened the room, although it too was faded.

There was a trunk situated beneath the tapestry in which Patches kept her extra clothing, and a small round table with a chair sat in the center of the room. A smaller square table in the corner displayed only one item. It was her great-grandmother's hand-carved wooden hairbrush, which had been handed down to Anna and then to Glenna. Glenna passed it down to each of her daughters and when Patches married, she would give it to the eldest of Justin's daughters. For now, it remained in her safekeeping and she often tried to imagine what the woman, who died in a plague, must have been like. It was rumored that she had an affair with the King of England, but that rumor was carefully kept in the family.

Patches picked up the brush and for the first time wondered if perhaps her great-grandmother married the wrong man. Be he Scot or English, a man was still a man, and there was no accounting for which a woman would truly love, or so Patches had been told. Yet considering her great-grandmother's dilemma held no answer to her own burning question—how was she ever to know if a man truly loved her?

Her contemplation was abruptly interrupted by a knock on the door and she quickly set the brush down. "You may enter."

Before she became Justin's wife, Deora spoke only English and had it not been for the wise ancestors who insisted the MacGreagors be taught English, she would have struggled to communicate. Yet even after years with her Scottish family, some words were beyond her and she often came to ask Patches to interpret.

Deora's smile was always warm, her dark hair carefully brushed and braided, and her blue eyes, which occasionally danced with conspiracy, portrayed her good health. Justin often said it was his wife's plotting that kept him young and everyone knew the two of them enjoyed their matchmaking best of all.

Deora gave her sister-in-law a quick hug. "What is the Gaelic word for the little loaves of bread?" She made a circle with her thumbs and forefingers touching.

"Bannock."

"Of course, I should know that one by now." She was about to say something else when a second knock on the door interrupted them.

"Enter," said Patches.

Justin did not often come into her bedchamber and as soon as she saw the look on his face, Patches knew something was wrong. "What?"

He put an arm around his wife and then turned to face his sister. He could think of no kind way to say it, so he just blurted it out. "Brevie has passed."

Patches could not believe her ears and she reached for Justin's arm to steady herself. "What happened?"

"Donan found her in the woods with an injury to the back of her head."

"She fell?" Deora asked, tears already beginning to form.

Justin put his other arm around his little sister. "Nay, she did not fall."

"Do you mean she was slain?" asked Deora.

When he nodded, Patches moved away, sat down on her bed, bowed her head and let the tears rim her eyes. "I cannot believe it. Who would do such a thing?"

"I do not know, but I intend to find out. Sister, you were seen talking to her at the loch; did she say she feared someone?"

Patches tried to remember. "Nay, we talked of taking husbands. Poor, poor Brevie." Patches rested her head in her hands for a moment. "But are you certain she did not fall or..."

"She was face down when Donan found her, and when he took me to the place in the forest, we discovered a tree branch with blood on it. Did anyone hate her or wish her harm?"

Patches shook her head. "If they did, I hardly think they would confide in your sister. Does everyone know?"

"Aye, they gather in the courtyard." He held his wife for a long moment and let her cry. "Will you stay with Patches?"

Deora wiped the tears off her cheeks. "Aye."

Justin let go of his wife, leaned down and kissed the top of Patches' head. "You must not go see her body, neither of you. I command it. No lass should have such a memory in her mind for all times. Will you give me your word not to go?"

"But once her body is washed and laid out, it is expected. What will they think if I do not go?" asked Patches.

Justin walked to the door, opened it and then stood there for a moment. "Mother could not be prevented and at the sight, began to cry so hard her breath left her. I feared we would lose her too and I'll not chance losing a wife or a sister because of it."

"Is her injury that unsightly?" Deora asked.

Justin did not answer. He simply closed the door behind him and then leaned against the staircase wall. His shock and grief was beginning to turn to rage. Only a warrior had the strength to crush Brevie's head in so completely. A MacGreagor had done this, he was certain of it, and if it was the last thing he ever did, he would find him out and execute him.

THE BURIAL WAS A SOMBER affair in more ways than one. With the clan following and a MacGreagor plaid draped over the top, six men carried Brevie's box from her cottage, through the courtyard and down the path to the graveyard. As he always did, the priest kept his voice soft and tried to comfort both her immediate family and the clan with his words. For her father, there was no comfort and he openly sobbed.

While they grieved the loss of Brevie in the days that followed, they were well aware her murder occurred not that far from the village, and it was unlikely an unfamiliar man could have gotten past the guards in broad daylight without being seen. It was possible, but not likely. Every woman looked at every man a little differently than before, trying to see some hint of guilt. The gossip was incessant with several placing the blame on different men for as little as an odd look. One thing they all agreed upon—the sooner he was caught, the sooner they could go back to their boring, but safe lives.

Justin forbade the women to go into the forest without at least two other women or a man for protection. Husbands kept better guard over their wives and daughters, who were happy to have it, and everyone paid more attention to their surroundings.

CHAPTER V

SHE SHOULD NOT HAVE, but Patches was so forlorn, she absentmindedly started into the forest. For two days, she took walks down the glen with one woman or another, let them cry on her shoulder and held back her own tears. She needed to grieve too.

They had not been the best of friends, true, but Patches would never have wished her to die and now...now, she would never know what Brevie could not forgive her for. She should have gone after her that day at the loch, made her tell and offered an apology. Not knowing what it was, had become a plague on her soul and seemed all she could think about. She could ask a member of Brevie's family, but it was too soon and too grievous to say how Brevie hated her. No, it was a question that would have to wait.

"Patches!"

The low voice of a man made her jump, put a hand over her heart and spin around. "I..."

Donan frowned. "Did your brother not say a lass is forbidden to go into the forest alone?"

"You frightened me."

"I meant to. 'Tis not safe here."

Patches squared her shoulders and glared at him. "I am not afraid, who would dare harm Justin's sister?"

"You were frightened enough just a moment ago." He took her elbow and guided her back toward the glen. "Truly, Patches, until we know who killed her, you must not be out here alone. The clan does not need more grief and some, I dare say a few, would grieve the loss of you."

She caught the glint in his brown eyes and smiled. "A few, is it? Perhaps you would care to name them."

"Well, your mother for one." As soon as they reached the edge of the forest, he let go of her elbow and clasped his hands behind his back.

"Go on, who else?"

"I fear no other name comes to mind just now."

She rolled her eyes and looked away. Donan was an unusually handsome man and she wondered why she had not noticed his wavy blond hair and thick beard before. If she wanted a husband, which she didn't, she might be tempted to consider him. "As I recall, you are five or six years my elder. Why have you not yet taken a wife?"

Again he was surprised at how direct Patches could be. Until Justin married, their laird was very protective of his sisters, not letting even the best of men near them. A wife changed that for the older sisters, but Patches was the baby in the family. Justin did not openly forbid talking to her, but a look of disapproval could keep a man well away. Just in case, Donan looked around to make sure Justin was not somewhere nearby frowning at him. He wasn't. "I am six years your elder and I have not yet found a lass with your beauty who tempts me."

Patches wrinkled her brow and not until he smiled, did she realize he was teasing her. "I should not have asked."

"Nay, you should not have. A wise man is very careful whom he chooses and must sometimes wait for the younger lasses to grow up. His heart must not be so easily stolen as that of a lass."

"Truly? I have heard the opposite. I have heard that a lad falls in love far faster than a lass. Is that not why the lad has to do all the persuading?"

He stopped walking and scratched the side of his beard. "Is that why? Are you quite certain?"

"I am not certain at all. What do I know of love and such things? I am yet a child."

He smiled. "But perhaps you would grow up quickly if you did not fear choosing the wrong husband."

"Perhaps so, you said yourself there is no way to tell and a life with the wrong lad is unthinkable."

"You are right and I see now I should not take a wife either. A lass may want me just for my charms alone and no lad can be charming always. On the other hand, all lads want sons to carry on his name and without a wife..."

Patches took a deep breath and let it out. "A wife might give you nothing but daughters."

"That is possible, but most lads are willing to chance it." At the sight of Justin and Shaw riding into the glen, he quickly half-bowed to Patches and walked away.

So caught up in her time walking with him, she only just realized they were in the middle of the meadow near the practicing warriors. She watched Donan join the others and begin to practice his sword fighting. They were always careful not to cut each other and their movements were slow at first, becoming steadily faster and more combative. It was something Patches had watched all her life and no longer found fascinating. At length, she went back to the Keep and the solitude of her bedchamber.

THEY DID NOT OFTEN ride together, and Justin was sad he could not take his best friend and brother-in-law with him to see the king. Nevertheless, Shaw was his second in command, a very wise man and the one Justin trusted most to care for the clan in his absence. Together they walked their horses toward the practicing men and then halted.

Justin was not there to see that the warrior practice went well; he was there to guess which were the strongest of his men. His brother-in-law, Ginnion, was more than equipped to teach the younger men and Justin could find no fault in the training. Still he watched, wondered and tried to see who might have the strength to kill Brevie so brutally.

Finally, he turned his horse and walked him on down the glen. "It could have been any one of them."

Shaw MacGreagor was nearly as big as Justin, had the same dark hair and blue eyes, yet his face was square and he preferred to wear his beard a bit longer than most other men. "Aye, they are all strong lads."

"I hate the thought that a MacGreagor killed Brevie."

"As do I, but all lads have tempers. She said or did something to enrage him."

"Or he forced her and then made sure she could not tell."

"That would be my guess too. But we did not let the lasses help with the washing and her mother is too upset to say."

"Should I ask her?"

Shaw shook his head. "Would knowing why help us find him out?"

"You are right, it would not help." Since the day he brought Deora to the village, Justin vowed to ride atop the hill as often as possible, just to look over the land and admire the beauty. He started up the gradual incline and did not speak again until he reached the top, turned his horse around and Shaw caught up with him. "The king commands me to bring five unmarried men and at first, I thought to take the ones I admire most. Now I wonder if I should take those that are the most dangerous."

"To marry Bethal?"

"There is that fret too. But I would fret less about the clan if the lads most quick to anger were with me."

Shaw rubbed the back of his neck thoughtfully. "Then we must choose five, but I can think of more than five and some are married."

"The king did not say five and only five. I will take them all and say they are my protection."

"How far is it to the King's castle?"

"Less than three days in good weather and if we do not stop often. But I journey so seldom, I see no need to rush. It will give me time to fish, get to know them better and perhaps provoke one or two. Tell me, which do you think are the most likely to kill a lass."

"I say we ask Ginnion. He works with them daily and he will know."

"You are right. I will take Donan too; if anyone can help me catch the killer, it is the lad who discovered her body." For several minutes, Justin looked out across the land he loved. Two of the horses in the glen below began to run, no doubt to escape a pestering bee. He was not concerned, all the horses were trained to come when called. With two men there to help if need be, a cow laid down to give birth while two new calves hurried to keep up with their mothers so they could nurse.

At length, Justin asked, "How many people might we lose this year?"

"The winter was harsh and the elders are weak. We lost five, though we made sure their fires were kept burning and they were well fed. Sixteen lasses are with child so far and we forever lose lads and lasses to injuries that will not heal."

"And one has been slain."

"Aye."

Justin narrowed his eyes and set his jaw. "I will kill the one who did it."

"And I will gladly help you."

A WARRIOR, A HUNTER and an occasional cabinetmaker, Donan did not often go inside the great hall and he was surprised when Justin sent for him. He entered and found his laird alone, standing in the middle of the room with his legs apart and his hands clasped behind his back.

"You will go with me to see the king." Justin said. He expected the man to be excited, but Donan was reluctant to say anything. It occurred to Justin he hardly knew the man. Of course he knew his name, who his parents were and what duties were assigned, but Donan was one of too many Justin had not gotten to know well. He made a mental note to change that in the future.

"Is it a command?" asked Donan.

"What is it? Why do you hesitate?"

"I do not care to be chosen by the king. I prefer to stay with the clan."

Justin could not fault the man for that. He considered telling Donan why he wanted him to go, but decided against it. "Perhaps you have found the lass you will marry here, am I right?"

"Perhaps."

"In that case, if you are chosen I will speak to the king on your behalf. Make ready, we leave in two days." Justin saw his nod, watched him walk out the door and considered which woman had caught the younger man's eye. While he saw nothing special in him, he'd heard several women comment on Donan's good looks. If it was true the king sought a Macgregor husband for Bethal, Donan had as good a chance as the others of being chosen. Justin took a deep breath and walked back to the table. He hoped he had not just promised Donan something he could not do—convince the king not to keep him.

THE DAY BEFORE HE WAS to depart with Justin, Donan made a point of waiting until Patches took her morning walk and then went after her.

There was a slight chill in the air and when she glanced up, storm clouds were gathering in the west. That's when she noticed Donan coming toward her. "Has my brother sent for me?"

"Nay."

"Then why do you follow?"

"Can you not guess?"

"You think I will walk into the forest alone again?"

"It would not be the first time." He bowed his head for a moment, raised it back up and then looked deep into her eyes. "I am to go with your brother. Promise I need not fret over you doing it again."

She found the earnestness in his eyes flattering, yet a bit uncomfortable. None of the men had been concerned for her safety in such a forthright manner before; at least not once she was grown. She brushed a strand of hair out of her face and broke the spell he had on her eyes. "If you wish."

"Say the words."

It was a command rather than a request, which left no doubt of his sincerity. "I promise, although you need not have asked. You managed to sufficiently frighten me and I have no intention of doing it again."

He smiled his relief, turned and walked away.

Patches glanced at the top windows of the Keep to make sure no one was watching. She sighed—no one was. If asked what Donan wanted, especially by Justin, she would have to confess she walked into the forest alone. She gladly set that worry aside and continued her walk.

Patches tried not to think about it, but it was odd that Donan was taking such a sudden interest in her. What did his concern mean? Perhaps he required that promise from all the women, but then, none of them were stupid enough to do what she had done. Was he showing a particular interest in her because she had become a woman? That thought both pleased and disturbed her. Not too long ago, she noticed him talking to Brevie. Was he the one Brevie was unsure of?

THEY WERE IDENTICAL twins of marrying age, yet both remained unmarried. They were, they feared, rather on the plain side where beauty was concerned, yet neither thought the other unsightly at all. Because they looked so completely alike, with curly brown hair that was often unruly, and big brown eyes and cheekbones that were perhaps a little too high, the elder of the two wore a broach pinned to the cloth over her heart. Two years older than Patches, each night they stood in the courtyard chatting, pretending not to notice and hoping a man would approach one and ask to walk with her. So far, none had.

Men and women often walked together during other hours of the day but it was not the same thing. Once a lass appeared in the courtyard, it was a signal that both she and her parents thought it was time for a husband. There were no such restrictions on the men and often a boy of twelve or thirteen would try his luck. The women thought it fun and never refused. After all, there would be ample time later for the boy to experience his first broken heart.

Both Catella and Jinty fancied Donan, but Donan had yet to even come to the courtyard even during the usual time for courting. At the end of each evening with no offers, they agreed they didn't care anyway. At least Donan had not chosen another and it was a great relief.

In the daytime when their chores were complete, the twins tried to be somewhere near Donan. Twice they even spoke to the man, but nothing ever came of it for either of them. Even so, they watched him like a hawk save for the times they had chores to tend.

When being near Donan was impossible, they enjoyed the company of Balloch. He was not as handsome, shorter than most men and as far as they were concerned, just a good friend. There was little the twins did not find out almost instantly about the clan's women, but from Balloch they learned about the men, and he was always willing to spread any gossip that came his way. He was a builder who normally applied his trade to the newest cottage. That made him easy to find, and he always greeted each twin with a smile and a nod.

Yet after Brevie's death, the women did not come to the courtyard nor did the men. Everyone was just too mournful. Then Justin took both Donan and Balloch with him to see the king, leaving the twins without a potential husband to pursue and a valuable source of gossip.

Catella, the eldest, sat down on a rock near the river and sighed. "I miss Balloch, he is very strong and he would protect us. I once saw him lift a log and toss it away. I tried, but I could not even lift it."

Jinty rolled her eyes, found a place nearby to sit, picked up a pebble and tossed it in the river. "I tried too, remember?"

"Of course I remember," said Catella, putting her nose ever so slightly in the air. "Sister, would you walk with Balloch if he asked you?"

"I would have to, wouldn't I? We must have a husband, even if it is Balloch."

"But you would rather it not be Balloch?"

"Why all these questions?" Jinty turned to look into her sister's eyes. "Do you prefer him? You do, do not deny it."

"I suppose I do. I did not before he went away, but I find I miss him. He is very kind and always helpful, but..."

"But what?"

Again Catella signed. "I fear he will choose you and not me."

"Then we must do something."

"What?"

"We must let him know you prefer him. We must start a rumor of our own."

"We cannot start a rumor of our own, it is unseemly," said Catella.

"Then we will ask Julie to help. She is very good at keeping secrets and will not say we asked her to start it."

"But Jinty, what if Balloch killed Brevie? How shall it be to marry such a lad?"

"Why do you suspect him? Is there something you have not said?"

Catella put her hands on her hips. "How am I to know something you do not know? We are always together."

"True."

"What if we never know who killed her?"

"I still say Stark did it, or maybe Luther. Or it could have been Ronan. He has a dreadful glare when he is riled," said Jinty.

"All men have dreadful glares."

Jinty suddenly drew in a sharp breath. "Suppose it was a lass who killed her?"

Catella shifted her eyes from side to side. "Do you think that is why Justin would not let us see her body and the men will not tell us how she died?"

"Could be, could very well be. She must have been all cut up on the face, but why would a lass kill her?"

Both were quiet for a moment and then guessed at the same time, "Donan."

"Aye," said Jinty. "Even we hated Brevie for that. She was always asking him to do this or that just to be near him, but who else wanted him?"

"Well, did we not see him talking to Patches yesterday?"

"Aye, but it was the first we've ever seen them talking and Brevie was already dead."

"But everyone knows Brevie and Patches hated each other. The day we saw Patches and Brevie talking at the loch is the first we've seen of it in years."

"Why did they talk just before Brevie died, I wonder," muttered Jinty.

"'Tis curious indeed."

"And what did they talk about?"

"Sister, we cannot think Patches killed Brevie, can we? She has never said a harsh word to either of us."

"You are right, it could not be Patches. Who else then?"

Catella tossed a pebble in the river and stood up. "Someone who is unmarried to be sure. I say we find her out."

"How?" Jinty asked struggling to get to her feet before her sister ran off.

"We will say we favor Donan and see what they do."

"But everyone already knows..." Jinty called to her sister as she watched her hurry up the path. "...that."

JUSTIN SPENT TWO NIGHTS in the forest with the eight men he chose to take with him and he saw no hint of guilt. If anything, he was beginning to get to know and like each of them. They were good protectors, loved to fish as he did and seemed to admire and respect him. It was what every laird hoped to see in his men. Their names were William, Ruskin, Andrew, Lonie, Balloch, Donan and the two married men were Rusell and Stark.

In no hurry by day, they stopped along the paths to hear the gossip from other clansmen and took in the sights of the rolling hills, peaceful lochs and distant mountains. They even paused to watch the swans fly west for the summer. Twice they happened upon a waterfall and thought to bathe, but the water was ice cold and none of them stayed in for long.

By campfire at night, they talked of wars, weapons and women. Two of the men were hunters and had far more stories to tell than the others. Occasionally in the past, Justin had a reason to send men to other clans to barter, but not often and these nine seemed delighted to be away from home and sharing an adventure with him. If one was a killer, Justin simply could not detect it.

BLUE INSTANTLY LIKED her and happily went to greet the woman Essen found walking alone in a clearing. The hour was late and she looked completely worn out. She carried a small sack of belongings over her shoulder and when she knelt down to pet the dog, she quickly closed the rip in her yellow and brown plaid. It was obvious her light brown hair had not been brushed recently and her eyes were dull and puffy from crying.

She accepted the dog's enthusiastic greeting, although she did not smile. When she finally noticed Essen, she tried to smile, but it was beyond her ability. She was not afraid of him and even hoped the man with the odd white clothing would kill her, for it would be a far better ending than the one she had already suffered.

Cautiously, Essen looked around for a husband or some other man who would certainly not be far away. The air was still, birds in the trees chirped as usual and he could smell no smoke from nearby campfires. At last, he decided there was no immediate danger and dismounted. "Blue sit." The dog quickly obeyed, but stayed within reach of her petting. "I am Essen MacKinnon. Is there no one with you?" He was surprised when she shook her head.

"Are you unwell?"

Except for aching feet and sore legs from walking, she guessed she was sound enough and shook her head.

"Are you hungry?"

The woman nodded and tried to think how long it had been since taking a meal. Too long, she realized. No wonder she had little strength left. "I am called Allie."

Essen set about building a small fire and then unpacked his barley and yeast. When he brought out his bowl and bone to grind the barley into flour, Allie came to him, took it out of his hands and sat down by the fire.

Essen smiled. "I saw a stream not far from here and I regret I did not fill my flask then. Blue will keep you safe and I will not be gone long. He quickly mounted and true to his word, he was only gone a few minutes.

He found three rocks about the same height and set them in a triangle in the fire. Then he unpacked a flat pottery slab to cook the barley on, set it on the rocks and as soon as Allie added the necessary amount of water and yeast to the barley, she poured part of the mixture on the slab.

She did not speak the whole time she prepared their meal, but seemed content to have something to do. It was not long after they ate, that he helped her make a bed out of her meager, worn out plaids. As soon as she was asleep, which took only seconds after she lay down, he spread his own blanket over her and then curled up in his rabbit skin cloak. At least it was a warm night and the rain was holding off. He was surprised when, instead of lying next to him, Blue was happy to sleep beside Allie.

SHE AWOKE FAR TOO EARLY, realized the stranger had not killed her as she hoped and dreaded yet another day of her misery. Allie closed her eyes but sleep would not come back and at length, she turned over and sat up. To her surprise, Essen was awake and already preparing hot cakes for their morning meal. They smelled wonderful so she got up, hurried into the trees to see to her comfort and then quickly came back.

She looked a great deal better than she had the night before and Essen was glad. "I am in need of supplies, is there a clan near?"

She seated herself, carefully tore off a piece of hot cake and tossed it from hand to hand, so she would not burn herself. "'Tis not far to the MacKeith hold. That is where I am going. It is my home…or was before I married a MacBain." With her bite of hot cake finally cool enough, she plopped it in her mouth and savored the taste. "I have been banished from the MacBains."

She said it so matter-of-factly it surprised him. He put the rest of the hot cake in his bowl and handed it to her. "Your husband has set you aside?"

"Not yet, but he soon will. I have no love for the lad, so it matters not."

Essen poured more batter onto his flat pan and got ready to flip it over with two sticks. "He should not have sent you away alone. You might have been set upon by any number of unworthy lads or wild beasts. I happened upon a wild boar just yesterday."

"My husband would prefer my death and so would I." She closed her eyes and slowly shook her head. "I did not kill him, but no one will believe me."

"Kill who?"

"My baby. He was but eight days old and the delight of his father, but two days hence, I awoke in alarm. The child had not cried in the night and when I lifted him out of the box, he was cold."

Essen noticed his dog snuggle up closer to the woman as if to comfort her. "How then are you to blame?"

Without thinking, she began to stroke Blue's head. "My husband claimed I did not want children and smothered the babe while he slept. He was right by half. I want children—just not his. I loved another when I was forced to marry." She forgot her meal, looked away and stared at nothing at all for a time. "Once I held the babe, I came to see he was the dearest thing in all the world, and something finally to love in my insufferable world. I could never harm him." Tears filled her eyes and began to roll down her cheeks. "I was not let stay for the burial. Laird MacBain put me out, closed the gate and charged me never to come back."

Essen knew not what to do or say, but he thought he should say something and finally remembered his father's words, "I am grieved to hear it."

She took a cloth out of her belt and wiped her eyes. "I do not want to go back. It is only that..."

"What?"

"I fear word has spread and my clan will not take me."

"Have you no family there?"

"I have a brother, if he yet lives."

"Perhaps you are wrong; perhaps your brother will be happy to have you back."

Allie wiped more tears away, took a deep breath and sighed. "I wish I could believe that. It was he who convinced me to marry a MacBain. He imagined they were a more plentiful clan and I would be happy. He was wrong and now look at me. The lad I love married another."

"Can a lass not love more than one lad?"

"Aye, but how will I know I have been set aside and am free to marry again? It is all so hopeless."

She hadn't touched the food so Essen tore off another piece of the hotcake in the bowl, blew on it and handed it to her. He had never considered what banishment might mean to a woman. It was bad enough for a man, but for a woman it was far worse. "I will take you to your home and if they will not have you, I will see you to a clan that will."

"Truly?" She remembered her hunger and took another bite. Then she really looked at him for the first time. He was an attractive man, tall and strong with kind eyes and a friendly smile. "Are you married?"

Essen was beginning to hate that question. In silence, he finished cooking the other hot cake and used the sticks to shove the pan away from the fire. "I am not married, nor do I wish to be. I must continue my search."

"What search?"

"I search for the golden sword."

She wrinkled her brow. "I heard of another lad who went in search of it and was never seen again."

Essen had not thought of that before. Suppose someone found it and it no longer remained where his father said to look. "Do you know in which direction he went?"

"North, I believe. He said the sword was in the north where all the giants live. Will you truly take me with you if I am sent away by my clan?"

"I will."

Allie breathed easier, got up and began to fold her bedding. "Then I best wash. 'Tis not far and we will be there by the noon meal. Can you take me back to that stream?"

CHAPTER VI

A forest fire could be extremely dangerous, but Justin and his men were out of the thick forest and had been for half a day. More often than not, a campfire was built using peat and once such a fire got out of control, the vegetation in the moor could burn for weeks. There were also wars between the clans over as little as a cow, a woman or a complete misunderstanding. So when they smelled smoke, they were determined to search it out. Cautiously, they rode their horses in the direction of the smoke, and it wasn't until they began to hear the shouts of men and the clash of swords that they knew it was a war.

Just before they reached the top of a hill, Justin held up his hand to stop them and then got down off his horse. He motioned for the others to follow, bent down and carefully moved closer to the crest. At length, he lay down and crawled until he could peek over the top.

Several of the cottages in the MacKeith village were on fire, and men on horses wearing dark blue kilts were tossing lit torches on the roofs of other cottages. The clan being attacked wore yellow and seemed scattered throughout the small village, yet they turned to fight whenever possible. Women and children ran for their lives while still more attackers moved in on foot. The small clan had little chance.

It wasn't long until the battle was over and it was then the reason for the massacre became clear. The attackers began to round up the livestock and herd them east, leaving only a meager assortment behind. There was little left to see and at length, the MacGreagors went back to their horses and continued north.

Once they were well away, William said, "We need a wall to protect us."

"Aye, but in a fire, a wall would trap us," said Stark.

Justin rolled his eyes. "He wondered how long it would take for that subject to come up." The MacGreagor clan once lived in a walled village. In fact, Justin was born there. Hidden doors made it possible for the people to get out if need be, but that village had no river behind it. Building a wall between the village and the river seemed unthinkable.

Yet the side with the river was where they were most vulnerable should another clan attack. Perhaps when he got home he would again hear the advice of the elders on that subject, and this time he would listen more carefully.

WITH ALLIE RIDING BEHIND him on his horse and Blue keeping pace next to Light, Essen halted to have a look around before they approached the village. No wonder Allie's brother encouraged her to marry a man from a more prosperous clan. From what Essen could see of the meadow, their livestock numbered only a few cows, a goat and three pigs. It was certainly not enough to feed more than a few people through a long winter.

He carefully looked through the sparse trees in all directions to make sure they had not been discovered, and then drew closer to the village. The wind shifted sending smoke their direction and it was far more smoke than normal hearths or outside campfires would make. Again he halted for a time just to watch and listen. Then, he slowly walked his horse closer until at last, he could see.

The MacKeith hold was the smallest Essen had yet seen and it had been attacked. Smoke still smoldered in two of the burned out cottages, and the men carrying buckets of water to put out the fires looked exhausted.

Women and children stood motionless, some with tears streaming down their cheeks. Others looked as though their disbelieving minds were lost in a haze. It appeared the dead of the attacking clan had already been taken away, if there were any, but the MacKeith dead remained on the paths with family members beside them mourning the loss.

"There!" Allie whispered leaning around Essen. She pointed to a man hauling water. "'Tis my brother, Ossian."

Cautiously, Essen guided his horse out of the trees and down the path to the village. He was well aware the MacKeith warriors might not welcome a stranger just now and was ready to draw his sword. When he thought they were near enough he halted, helped Allie slide down and then held his breath. He promised, but he did not truly want to take her with him. To his relief, her brother was thrilled to see her. He watched them talk for a moment, saw them embrace and when Allie nodded to him, Essen knew she was welcomed home.

Still, there was no hope of bartering for the fresh vegetables he longed for. This clan clearly needed all they had, so he slowly turned his horse and continued to make his way south.

AFTER SPENDING HALF a day of riding and the other half fishing, Justin and his men ate their fill, made their beds and then sat around the campfire talking. Justin thought to provoke his men just to see their reaction. "Perhaps Brevie deserved to die." Seated around the campfire, the men swore at the very idea and their upset was equally matched, in all except Donan who remained quiet.

Donan stared at the ground until the others calmed down. "No lass deserves to die that way. When I first found her, I confess I knew not what to do. If I took her home, her mother would have to see..." He paused to take a deep breath. "But leaving her there for one of the lasses to find was unthinkable too. She was clearly dead and I confess it took every measure of my strength to force myself to lean down and pick her up." Again, he paused to breathe deeply. "Her blood began to soak into my clothing as I carried her into the glen. I thought to take her to the Keep, but her father saw and came to me. If I live to be a thousand, I shall never forget the pain in his eyes. He took her out of my arms and soon other men surrounded him, so the lasses could not see. I held back and waited for what I knew would happen next. As soon as the door to the cottage was opened, her mother screamed. It was then I realized..."

While Donan described the awful event, Justin took a long look at each man's face. Still he could see no irregularities. All of the men held their eyes cast down and remained silent. Yet, he saw each clench his fists and struggle to hold back his urge to kill the one responsible. Could a man pretend such emotion if he did not actually feel it? Justin didn't believe so and was left with no other thought—the man who killed Brevie was not among the ones he brought with him.

At least now, he need not worry that Bethal would choose an unworthy man among the ones he brought. The question was, how quickly would she make her choice, if indeed that was what the king was up to, and how quickly could he get back home?

IT WAS THE EIGHTH VILLAGE Essen had come across since he left his home in the north. A couple of clans were friendly, but the others were not, causing him to complete his business as quickly as possible. Each time he asked about the golden sword and each time, he was told it was just a fable from long ago and not to be believed. He bartered for supplies, asked directions to the next clan and went on his way.

As he always did, when he came to the next village, he hid in the forest some distance away to watch. The people seemed harmless enough. They went about their duties, children played on the paths and the smell of baking bread filled the air.

Suddenly, he heard a woman scream.

THE MOMENT SHE SPOTTED him, Bethal ran the full length of the king's great hall and flew into Justin's arms. Shrieking with delight, she felt her laird lift her off the ground, swing her around and kiss her cheek.

"How much we have missed you." Standing in front of the king with his men lined up beside him, Justin put her down, held her at arm's length and looked her over. "I believe you have grown into the most pleasing lass I have ever seen."

She puffed her cheeks and playfully smacked his arm. "You say that to every lass you see, and let us not forget your wife is the most becoming of us all."

"Of that, she will not let me forget." He grinned and hugged her once more. "Do you remember...?"

"Of course I do." She began to greet the men one at a time. True happiness was being in the company of Justin and the most handsome MacGreagor men she had ever seen. She knew them and in fact grew up with them, but somehow they were different now. When her eyes met Donan's, she felt something she had never felt before. Her blush confused and embarrassed her, so she quickly nodded and moved to the next man. It was the first of several times she would glance his direction and he was always watching her.

"Balloch, you have grown taller since last I saw you and more handsome as well," said Bethal.

Always mindful of his smaller size, Balloch was more than pleased with her comment. "Have I? If that be the case, might I be allowed to take you for a walk in the morning? I have much news to tell you and..."

"So do I," Andrew said, joining his objection with the mumbling of the others. "We all do and it is no doubt the same news."

The king held up his hand to silence them. "What say you, Bethal? Shall I let them court you?"

Bethal turned around, lowered her head and looked at the king through the top of her eyes. "So that is what you are up to. What bribe have you offered to get them here?"

Unfamiliar with the banter between Bethal and the king, Justin held his breath and watched the king stand up, take off his crown, set it on a table and then shed himself of his red cloak. Soon he was standing next to Bethal facing Justin. "Bribery? My dear, no lad with his wits about him, needs to be bribed to be in your company. I would never allow it."

Noticing his alarm, Bethal winked at Justin to comfort him. "Do you suppose they are all out of their wits, then?"

The king chuckled and looked at Justin. "How have you managed to send me such a suspicious lass?" Yet the king did not allow him time to answer and instead turned his attention back to Bethal. "I believe you have avoided answering the question."

"My king, are you aware three are already married? Did you not promise to have a marriage set aside if I prefer one of them?"

Justin raised both eyebrows and shock crossed the faces of the other two married men. "Of course," Bethal quickly added, "I could never desire someone else's husband, so they are safe." She thought she could actually see all three heave a sigh of relief. Bethal smiled and then turned back to face the king. "What was the question?"

The king rolled his eyes. "Will you take a walk with these lads in the morning or not?"

"Do you insist?"

"I do."

Bethal tipped her head to one side. "And my duties?"

"You have no duties until these lads take their leave. They are family, or so you often tell me. Enjoy them while you may."

"Well, I *would* like word of my family and friends."

Justin's heart sank. He was certain word of Brevie's death had not reached Bethal and he should be the one to break the bad news. He considered telling her right away and then decided against it. Bethal could not choose a husband with tears in her eyes, it might take days for her to recover and he did not intend to stay that long. There would be time to tell her before they started home.

Playfully, Bethal looked the unmarried men up and down with a discerning eye—all except Donan, which Donan noticed and so did

Justin. "I fear, my king, that if I am forced to see them one at a time, I should be walking nearly all day long. Perhaps I may see them all at once."

The king frowned. "All at once? I hardly think you can get to know them all at once."

"But you forget, I already know them. They are all good lads and I suspect the best of the lot or Justin would not have brought them." She detected just a slight swell in the chests of two of the men.

On the outside, she was playing the game with the king but inside she was upset. "Tell me, Laird MacGreagor did these volunteer or were they forced to come."

"I confess I chose them, but they have not objected. Each has agreed to stay in the king's service if chosen."

"I see, they have been offered a fine position. But I must wonder, who is to choose which will stay?" she asked.

"I do not know," Justin answered.

Bethal again turned her suspicious eyes on the king. "You did not tell them marriage to me is the price they must pay?"

The king winced, looked at her and then at Justin. "Good heavens, did my messenger not say?"

Justin was about to answer when Bethal interrupted. "I believe the harm is already done. There, you see, because they did not know, they are *not* honor bound to court me."

"You dismiss them quite easily, Bethal," said the king. "You have forgotten they made the request before they knew of the condition. I say give it your best. If you find one suitable, I am willing to let you visit the MacGreagors twice a year—more if you insist. There, that should satisfy even your suspicious mind."

The king took her hand, wrapped it around his arm and walked her toward the table. "It is late, the queen waits to be let in and I say we feed these hungry sojourners, and then send them off to their rest. I've beds aplenty in the upper chambers and they will be saved from another night on the hard ground. Tomorrow they will draw lots to see whom will be first and if you so choose, you may simply sit with one or two instead of walking. That's an end to it, my dear; I will hear no more objections." He motioned to his guard, waited until the large double doors opened and then went to greet the queen and her attendants.

THE QUEEN DISTRACTED Bethal just long enough for Justin to tell his men not to mention Brevie, and then seated her ladies, one each next to a man to make the conversations more lively. It was a fine meal with more food than even the hearty MacGreagor warriors could comfortably eat. When the meal was finished and the queen spoke up, they all quieted.

"Tell me, Laird MacGreagor, how have you managed to marry an English?" asked the queen.

Justin smiled. "I believe she used trickery, my queen."

The queen's eyes danced with excitement. "Trickery? Do tell us."

"She pretended to hate me," Justin said.

"Ah," the queen began, "A handsome laird is not accustomed to being rebuffed. How clever of her, was there another she preferred?"

Bethal giggled. "Nay, 'twas her father who kept betrothing her, first to a lord and then to a duke she had never once laid eyes on. And had my laird not married her, I know of several others in our clan who would have. Deora is the delight of all who know her."

"Aye," said the king, "but she *is* English."

The room went deadly still and everyone waited to see who would speak. The Scots and the English hated each other, and to befriend the English, let alone marry one, was not forbidden, but was usually frowned upon.

Justin never took his eyes off the King's. "Aye, but she hides it well." He watched and waited until the king began to smile.

"Does she learn Gaelic or have you learned English?" the king asked.

"My grandmother was also English. She taught my father and he taught me. We once lived much closer to the English, and my father reasoned that being able to understand an enemy could win a war."

The king took a sip of his wine and thought about that for a long moment. "Of course, I remember now. Your father was Neil Mac-Greagor. Do you know what truly happened when the MacDonalds attacked? I have heard many a story, but I cannot be certain which to trust."

"I was not yet two when it happened, but I will tell you what I have heard." Justin scooted his chair back a little, folded his arms and began. "There was but one creek that ran through the land of the MacDonalds north of us. From there it crossed into our land, fed our moat and continued on into England. However, we had a loch and the MacDonalds did not. Laird MacDonald was forever damming the creek in an attempt to make a loch of his own. Naturally, my father objected."

The queen wrinkled her brow. "I see no harm in letting the MacDonalds have a loch of their own."

Justin nodded. "Neither did my father, but had the water dried up, the English would have come to find out why."

"Ah, I see," said both the king and the queen at nearly the same time.

"The old laird died and the new MacDonald laird coveted our land as well as our loch. It was a constant concern and father knew sooner or later the MacGreagors would have to fight to keep their home. We were more than a thousand strong and could have soundly taken the MacDonalds save for one thing."

"Which was?" asked the king.

"The plague. It cut our numbers in half while the MacDonald clan fared much better. When war came, they were twice our number. Our village had a wall around it and…"

"But you had hidden doors in the wall," said the king.

"True, but by then the secret of the doors was no longer a secret and when they attacked, the MacDonalds were outside the doors waiting. We might easily have been trapped, but guessing the day would come, father dug a tunnel for our escape."

"Then there was a tunnel. As I recall, there was also a great fire. Am I mistaken?" the king asked.

"Indeed there was a fire. Father had a fine keep and declared no MacDonald would ever sleep in his bedchamber. So just before the escape, he set the village and the Keep on fire."

The queen's jaw dropped. "Is this the land all of Scotland believes is haunted?"

Bethal started to giggle. "Aye, that's the one. The MacDonalds thought the MacGreagors had burned themselves alive. But families also lived outside the wall and the MacDonalds managed to capture some of our women. The lasses then made up fables about seeing dead MacGreagors walking the paths at night." She paused and took a long breath.

Said the king, "Go on, what happened next?"

"Well, the MacDonalds grew so tired of lasses screaming in the night and swearing they saw the ghost of a MacGreagor, that Laird MacDonald gave our lasses all they wished and sent them away."

"There, you see my love," said the queen, "lasses are just as clever as men given the occasion."

The king smiled, "I believe they are. Nevertheless, after we have completed this day, I shall vow I never said that." He enjoyed their laughter and then nodded to Bethal. "Have you a desire to play?"

As she always did, she stood up, curtsied and rushed to the side of the room to get the Slype-Groat board. Yet, to play in front of the men in her clan made her self-conscious and unsure. She and the king exchanged the usual banter, but she glanced too often at Donan and the king noticed. After an hour or two of play, she conceded her loss.

The king was overjoyed, not because he won the game finally but because the odds that his Bethal would marry one of these men and stay in his company were good, very good indeed.

AS THEY ALWAYS DID, whistles down the length of the long glen alerted the MacGreagors that a stranger was coming. It was a welcome interruption. However, the stranger on a white horse with a dog running alongside seemed in a big hurry to get to them, and the closer he got the more alarmed the whistles became. Something was amiss and the two men Justin left in command, Shaw and Ginnion, quickly mounted their horses and rode out to meet the stranger.

At first, the man seemed to be alone, but as they drew nearer, they could clearly see he held someone in his lap wrapped in a rabbit skin cloak. The closer they got, the worse the woman looked. Shaw urged his horse to gallop and when he got closer still, he put his hand up to stop the stranger and then halted beside him. Both her eyes were bruised and nearly swollen shut. Her lip was split and she appeared more dead than alive. For a long moment, he studied the woman and then glared at the man. "Have you done this?"

"Nay, her husband did it."

"Who is she?"

"She says her name is Trallen MacGreagor."

Shocked, Shaw glanced at Ginnion, looked at the woman again and tried desperately to recognize her. "Trallen? She is sister to..."

Ginnion quickly moved his horse up on the other side of the stranger and lifted his sister into his arms, rabbit cloak and all. He kissed her forehead, turned his horse around and raced toward the village shouting commands as he went.

Shaw watched him go and then turned his attention back to the stranger. "There will be an uproar in our clan this night. She is much loved. Is she hurt inside?"

"I have seen no evidence of it, but the damage was done when I got there and I did not take the time to look for other injuries."

Shaw walked his horse around Essen's and together they continued on toward the village at a leisurely pace. "When her husband comes for her, I will see that he dies for this."

"He will not come; I killed him."

Shaw nodded. "Good, you have saved me the trouble. You did well to bring her home. What is your name?"

"I am Essen MacKinnon."

"Essen? I have heard this name before. The MacKinnons are...they are..." He hesitated to say it.

"Heathens? Indeed they are."

"I should like to hear of this clan. Would you enjoy a fine meal and a day of rest with us?"

"Aye, but I best go back and bury her husband before he is discovered."

"Bury him? Let his own people bury him."

"Aye, but if I do not, they will think his wife killed him. Will they not want her returned so they can avenge his death?"

Shaw thought about that. The MacGreagors would never give Trallen back and a war with the Kennedys was not a pleasant thought. He had no doubt the MacGreagors were a much stronger clan and would win, but he was not anxious to go to war just now—not with Justin off to see the king. "I will send men to help you."

Essen watched Ginnion slide down off his horse in the courtyard and carry his sister into the Keep. MacGreagors were already gathering and as word spread of who the woman was, he could see some gasp and others bow their heads. "Nay, I killed him and I alone will do the burying."

"As you wish, do you know that clan?"

"Nay, I was about to enter the village when I heard her scream."

"They are Kennedys and they are not to be trusted. We should not have let her marry him. Will you come back then? Trallen's family will want to thank you."

"I will come back." Essen halted his horse, returned Shaw's nod and then looked toward the courtyard once more. A young woman stood near a short stonewall paying no attention to the others. Instead, she was looking directly at him. He could not remember ever seeing a more pleasing woman. Her long hair curled around her face with part hanging down the front and the rest, he guessed, down her back. Suddenly, he was anxious to get the burying done and come back, if for no other reason than to get a closer look at the woman.

Essen let Blue jump into his lap, turned his horse around and headed back down the glen.

HE COULD HAVE USED help with the burial, but he needed time alone more. There was a thing that weighed heavy on Essen's mind and he wanted to sort through his feelings. Killing a man who deserved to die was one thing, but the rage with which Essen killed greatly surprised him. His fury was complete and he hit the man in the face with such force, he felt the man's jaw break. If that were not enough, he picked the smaller man up and bodily threw him out the door of the cottage. Then he drew his sword and before he realized he had not allowed the man to draw his weapon, the killing was finished. Essen looked down at the lifeless body for countless moments before he remembered the woman and went back inside to help her. After that, his only concern was getting her home alive and he had no time to think. It was all she could do to tell him which way to go and he feared she would die before he found her home.

Now he could not stop thinking about what he had done. It was not the first time Essen felt anger, but never had his anger turned to such rage. It frightened him, and if it frightened him, he was certain to frighten others.

CATELLA AND JINTY WERE exhausted. In unison, they sat down on a log near the graveyard and tried to think. Jinty swore that when their naturally curly red hair became especially unmanageable, it meant a very bad storm was on the way. Catella thought that was nonsense.

Nevertheless, half the morning Jinty struggled to get her hair braided and eventually gave up. Why not give up, she thought, Donan was not there and no other man was likely to notice her. "I wager he will not come back."

"Who?" asked Catella.

"The lad in white."

"Oh him. I did not think him handsome and besides, is he not the one in white Balloch said was daft?"

Catella wrinkled her brow. "So he did. Yet he brought Trallen home, so he must have some wits about him."

"All lads have *some* wits about them."

"Oh sister, what are we to do?"

"About what?" asked Jinty.

"We have talked to every unmarried lass in the clan and none confess to killing Brevie."

"Aye, but at least we found out how she died. Do you suppose everyone knew but us?"

"It would seem so," said Catella.

"I wonder what else we do not know."

"We do not know how to catch a husband."

Jinty sighed. "Aye, who could have imagined it to be so hard?"

CHAPTER VII

WHILE THE FIRST OF the unmarried men took his turn walking with Bethal, Justin and the others were given a tour of the castle, and then taken into each guard tower to enjoy the view of the sprawling rolling hills and the warrior encampment. Scattered cottages dotted the farmland and even a small village or two could be seen in the distance. Justin and the king chatted about the war between the Kennedys and the Swintons, which led Justin to explain how he happened to have an English wife in greater detail.

The king smiled and led the way down the steps of the forth guard tower. "My wife captured my love in less than ten minutes. It seems to have taken you a while longer. Perhaps you are a more cautious lad."

"Or a more stupid one. Now I cannot think what I would do if I lost her."

"I shall pray you do not, though I cannot promise God hears the prayers of all kings." He flashed his grin at the other two men, led them into a sitting room on the second floor of the castle and found his favorite chair. "Now MacGreagor, send your lads off to their pleasures and tell me what weighs so heavily on your mind? Is there to be another war? A plot against me? Or perhaps you are simply eager to take your leave."

Justin nodded for his men to leave, closed the door behind them and with the king's permission, seated himself on a chair opposite. "You are as wise as I have heard. I confess I am eager to go home, but not for the reason you imagine. A lass was slain just before we came and I have not yet discovered the slayer. Brevie was as dear to us as Bethal. In fact, they were close friends and I have not yet told Bethal. I did not wish to…"

"Upset her just now? I quite understand. You fear the blackguard may kill again and you should be there to stop him. I dare say, it may happen even with you there."

"I cannot argue with that." Justin leaned forward, put his elbows on his knees and ran the fingers of both hands through his hair. "The lad who did this hit her with far more force than was necessary to cause her death. If I am there, I might discover him before he kills again."

"Aye, but we can hardly expect Bethal to fall in love in only one day. You will stay until the end of the week. We should know by then which she prefers."

THE LAST TO ASK FOR Bethal's attention in the small first floor sitting room of the castle was Donan and she was surprised. The queen said the king sent for only five and she secretly hoped Donan was one of them, but when he was not, she was disappointed. She was about to leave when he softly knocked, opened the door and walked to her.

"You look tired," he said, not bothering to take a seat.

"Do I?" she asked. "It is perhaps too much excitement for one day."

"Then we must find a place to sit outside in the sunshine. I saw a large rock not far from the courtyard where children were at play earlier."

"I know it well and I am quite fond of resting there." She let him open the door for her, stepped out and led the way down the stone path to the rock.

This late in the day, the place was void of children and was instead peaceful and quiet, with only a gentle breeze rustling the spring leaves in the trees. He held out his hand, helped her sit and then sat down beside her, although not too close. "I used to watch you play stones with the laddies. You were quite good."

She blushed. "Good heavens that was a lifetime ago. Was I a dreadful child?"

"Indeed you were, you would not let the laddies win even once."

"Aye and after a time they refused to play with me."

"I believe you took up sword fighting after that hoping to skewer a laddie or two."

Bethal giggled. "Aye, but Justin would not let me play with a real sword. He was most cruel and I told him so."

"What did he have to say to that?"

"I believe he said the punishment for hurting one of his future warriors was to clean up after the horses. I was immediately cured of my vengeful intentions." Donan's smile lit up his whole face and it touched her so, she could hardly look at him.

"Tell me, have you found the one you will marry among the MacGreagor men?" he asked.

"How shall I possibly choose? They are all such fine lads."

"Indeed they are, but perhaps you might prefer one or two more than the others?"

"Perhaps," she admitted.

"Is it Rusell?"

"How odd you should ask about him first."

"Is it? I should think his attachment to you was evident to all of us last night."

Bethal looked down and began to toy with a fold in her skirt. "He is a good lad, to be sure, and he made mention of it several times. His list of accomplishments is quite long and...well...he..."

"Go on, he what?"

"The truth be told, the lad does not stop talking of his accomplishments."

"I see, and what of the others?"

"Lonie and Andrew had very little to say for Rusell had already told me all the news. William, on the other hand, cared not that I had already heard most of it, was full of news of home and could not stop talking. I believe I might have said only two words the whole time he walked with me. But Balloch was the most interesting."

"You prefer Balloch?"

"Not at all and that is what made him so interesting. He does not prefer me either. He loves another, you see. Oh he is quite willing to be in the King's service, but he hoped to marry and bring his wife here."

"He was the first to ask to walk with you."

"Aye, but he did not mean it that way."

Donan smiled. "So Balloch is in love? I had no idea, is it one of the twins?"

"Jinty and Catella?"

"Aye."

"I asked him the same and he nodded so I promised not to choose him." Bethal giggled. "Never have I seen such relief on a man's face. He became so excited, he nearly fell over a chair on his way out of the sitting room."

Donan smiled, shifted his position and crossed his feet at the ankle. "Will you be happy staying here?"

"Until yesterday I had not considered it. I fully intended to go home when my time was up, but as you see the king is a difficult lad to refuse."

"He is certainly fond of you. If he were not married, he might..."

"Aye, but he is married and happily so. I am his entertainment and that is all."

"But if something happened to the queen, would you desire him?"

Bethal studied the serious expression on his face. "Desire a lad older than my father?"

"Such has happened before and quite often. Besides, he could make you a queen."

"A queen? I had not thought of that."

"All lasses covet being the Queen of Scots and who could blame them?"

"If they do, 'tis because they know no better. She is admired, to be sure, but hers is not always a happy life and I would not want it."

"Why not?" he asked.

"I want to be free to go riding, to swim in the loch when the weather permits and to not always be surrounded by people. The queen hardly has a moment of her own. Her duties are endless, what with choosing which food to serve at meals, and..."

"Then what sort of life do you want?"

Bethal took a moment to breathe and think. "I want to live in a cottage with a husband who loves me...and is not bribed to marry me."

"You mean with so little as a position in the king's service?"

"Precisely."

"Then you will choose none of these?"

"How can I? Think of it Donan, a position in the King's guard would be enthralling for any lad. He will escort the king all over Scotland, know all the kings business and be included, possibly, in helping the king make decisions. Pretending to love me would be a very, very small price to pay."

"What will you do then?"

"I want to go home."

"So do I," he said.

"You do? You do not desire a position with the king?"

"Nay, Justin bid me to come and when I said I would rather not, he pledged to have a word with the King if I am chosen."

"I see."

Both of them were quiet for a time, each lost in thought. Then Donan broke the silence. "It would be unkind to walk with the men daily with no intention of choosing one of them."

"True." Again, she studied his expression. "Do you wish to go home because you are in love? Is it Brevie? She would make a good wife, she thinks you quite handsome."

He had not expected her to mention Brevie and had to look away. "Nay, I am not in love."

"Nor am I." Bethal got up, walked to a tree, turned around and leaned her back against the trunk. Spring flowers were just beginning to bloom in the gardens, but wild bluebells seemed to have sprung up overnight. "This is unpleasant for us all. The king has many powers, but making people fall in love is not one of them."

When the breeze moved the leaves and let the sun shine on her face, he found her even more pleasing. "There is only one answer?"

"What?"

"Do you enjoy a bit of intrigue?"

"Everyone likes intrigue. Go on, what have you in mind?"

"Well, we could pretend we have taken a liking to each other."

"Reject the others, you mean? But how shall I tell them?" she asked.

"I will tell Justin our intrigue and he will see to it."

"Very well, but the king will expect us to spend considerable time together."

"You have been relieved of your duties and I appear to be free, so why not? We could go riding, so long as we stay within sight of the guards and the king gives his permission."

"Then there are long walks in the morning, games in the afternoon and we will spend evenings with the king and queen." She pondered the idea for a moment. "But then what? You are to leave soon."

"You could say you do not find me suitable after all. I shall look wounded, naturally. Then you can serve the rest of your time here and go home as you planned."

Her grin widened. "'Tis a wonderful idea. I do so want to go home and your intrigue will persuade the king to stop trying to marry me off—hopefully."

ESSEN SPENT FOUR DAYS considering what he had done. After burying Trallen's husband, he tried to make certain he was not being followed by traveling in one direction, doubling back and then going another way. Exhausted finally, he found a small clearing and rested. The next three days, he bathed, fished, took long walks and tried to calm himself. Yet he was still troubled and found no answer to his burning question—how does a man control that kind of rage?

Perhaps there was no answer; perhaps he was simply doomed to be a frightening sort of man.

Essen had not forgotten the woman he wanted to see up close and thought about her often. By the end of the fourth day, it was as though she somehow called to him. Besides, he wanted to know if Trallen had survived as well as recover his cloak. So he gathered his things, mounted his horse and set out.

The second time he entered the long, wide MacGreagor glen, it was with much less urgency. He heard the whistles announcing his arrival and wondered if the two men would once more come to meet him. Blue often got tired of running and was let up on the horse, but on this day, the dog spotted a cat, sat up and leapt off the horse to chase it. It was Blue's first encounter with a common house cat and Essen paused to watch. It didn't take long for the cat to stop, face its pursuer, spit and swat Blue in the face. The dog yelped and took up a less threatening position by lying down and rolling over on his back. It made Essen laugh.

The glen looked oddly familiar but he thought nothing of it. Everywhere, except on the path leading to the village, a sea of blue spring flowers coated the floor of the meadow. Grazing livestock, some with new calves or colts, ignored his arrival although one mare seemed interested in his stallion. It was clearly spring, all things were becoming renewed and the sight of it lifted his spirits.

He urged his horse on toward the village still plagued with the feeling he knew the place. Perhaps it was only because he had been there before. As he hoped, by the time he drew near the courtyard, Shaw, Ginnion and another man came to meet him, only this time on foot. As soon as they were near, Essen slid down off his horse.

"We are pleased you have come back," said Shaw, who then nodded toward the elder third man. This is, Ben. He is Trallen's cousin and he will be pleased to brush your horse and feed him.

Essen let Ben take the reins and began to walk with Shaw and Ginnion toward the Keep. "Light will be most grateful."

"Light? You named your horse Light?" asked Ginnion.

"'Tis a long story."

"In that case, you must stay long enough to tell it." Shaw said.

"How is Trallen?" Essen asked.

"Better," said Ginnion. "She says she does not hurt inside and the bruises to her face and head are healing."

Essen let out the breath he didn't realize he'd been holding, "Good, I was worried."

"Our laird is away just now, but his family is here and they are eager to meet the lad named Essen," Shaw said.

"Why?"

"Our elder mistress, Glenna, tells stories about the land of Essen."

He was surprised to hear that. Two little boys and a little girl raced out to meet him, but their interest was in his dog instead and when he looked behind him, Blue was on his back again letting the children rub his belly. People were scattered all up and down this part of the glen watching him and others were gathered in the courtyard. When he walked through the gap in the wall into the courtyard, men nodded and two women curtsied, which he thought was rather odd. What he noticed most was a set of identical twins who gawked at him, repeatedly cupped their hands and whispered in each other's ear.

Soon, he was ushered into the great hall where two serving women, Justin's wife, Deora, the elder mistress, Glenna, and her four daughters waited to greet him. Two of the daughters, Brenna and Carley, had dark hair with bright blue eyes, while the other two, Ceanna and Patches, had lighter hair the same color as their mother's. To his amazement, the woman he wanted to see up close was among them. Blue took one look at Patches, sprinted across the floor, jumped up and put his paws on her skirt.

"Blue!" commanded Essen. The dog instantly went back to sit at his owner's heels. "Do forgive..." Essen began.

Shaw could not contain his curiosity. "Am I to understand you have a horse named, Light, and a dog named, Blue?"

Essen smiled. "I see how it might seem odd, but it serves me well. Not long ago when I was put upon to marry a lass who held a dagger at my back, I simply said, 'light blue.' My dog came to protect me and my horse to take me away."

Patches joined her smile to the others. The stranger was even more pleasant looking up close and he seemed of good humor, a quality she much preferred. She nodded when she was introduced, but his eyes held hers for longer than was customary and she felt shy. That was a circumstance she was completely unfamiliar with and did not like at all. Suddenly irritated with his power over her, she silently vowed to hate him. "Which clan wears white?"

"Tis a very long story," said Essen.

Justin's mother took Essen's arm and guided him to the table. Glenna carried her age well, although her hair had turned gray and her cheeks were not as filled out as they once were. Wrinkles at the corners of her eyes deepened when she smiled. "We will hear your story, but first I must know from where you got the name Essen." She seated herself and folded her hands in her lap. "There was once a storyteller who..."

Entranced with Glenna's friendliness, he sat down before he remembered his aunt charged him to remain standing until the women sat, so he stood back up. "Was it a Larmont?"

Glenna's eyes widened. "I am a Larmont, or was before I married. Have you come from that clan? Shaw said you are a MacKinnon."

Essen waited for the other women to take a seat, sat back down and accepted the goblet of wine a serving lady handed him. He noticed the sisters were lined up on the other side of the table with Patches almost directly across from him. Two of their husbands took tall-backed chairs on his same side of the table and he wondered if that was customary. "My father was a Larmont. Do you remember the story of the Land of Essen?"

Patches rolled her eyes. "Remember it, she tells it every chance she gets."

"And you love it each time," Glenna shot back, "Unless you have outgrown it in the last few weeks."

"I *am* too old for stories," Patches said.

"I see," said her mother.

Quiet until now, no look between Essen and Patches went unnoticed by her eldest sister, Ceanna. "Perhaps if Patches would take a husband, she would have more to do than sit with the children and listen to your stories, mother."

Patches puffed her cheeks and looked at Essen. "Why is it that married lasses think unmarried lasses should be ever so happy as they are? I see no sense in it at all. I have a very large bedchamber upstairs, and all I will ever need just as I am now. If I marry, I will find myself in a small cottage, washing, cooking and cleaning. I have yet to see the advantages."

With the room so silent, Essen knew they were all waiting for him to answer, "I am afraid I have little experience with either married or unmarried lasses. But if you say you have no need of a husband, then I believe you."

It was not the reaction Patches was expecting and she quickly glanced at all the others watching her.

Seated next to Essen, Shaw was enjoying the exchange between them. "She was expecting you to try to change her mind as the rest of us have."

"Why would I do that? Is not a large bedchamber what all lasses want?" At first, he looked deadly serious, and it wasn't until Essen cracked a smile that the others laughed.

All laughed but Patches, who gave her brother-in-law a stern look and then turned her attention back to Essen. "Why have you so little experience with lasses?"

"Patches," Glenna scolded, "it is not proper to…"

"Mother," Patches interrupted, "he looks all grown up to me, let him answer."

Essen liked her. She was perhaps too easily annoyed, but he liked her just the same. "Why do they call you Patches?"

"You must answer my question first."

Essen took the bowl of mutton stew the server handed him and thought to take a bite before he answered, but according to his aunt, he was obliged to wait until the others began to eat. "I believe your mother wished to tell a story first."

"Indeed I did," said Glenna. "She began her story while they ate and although she touched little of her own evening meal, she got to the end just as the rest finished eating. "…and so the lovely lass became the Queen of Scots." Not once did Glenna or Essen notice that nearly every member of the family was feeding mutton to the dog under the table.

"Good, that is over with at last," said Patches. She dared glance at him several times while her mother talked, but he seemed so engrossed in the story, he did not once look at her. "'Tis time to hear your story, Essen."

He took a cloth out of his belt and cleaned his facial hair just in case stew had soiled it. "I am not as good a storyteller as your mother. Perhaps she might teach me first."

Patches set her bowl aside and folded her arms. "Are you always this unruly?"

"Aye."

The MacGreagor family could not contain their laughter. Patches, most of them guessed, had just met her match. Ginnion finally spoke up, "My sister-in-law's demands aside, I would like to hear your story. We receive such uncommon reports of the MacKinnons we tend not to believe any of them."

"While I did not live among them," Essen began, "I watched them often enough to doubt anything you heard is untrue. But perhaps I should begin at the beginning. My mother..."

She was annoyed, but the longer Essen spoke, the more drawn into his story Patches became. She smiled where it was appropriate to smile, looked shocked, as did the others at times and admired this little boy who grew to be a man all by himself. His manners were not as polished as others, but his ease of talking and increasing good looks were impossible to ignore.

Essen tried not to look at her often, but he could not seem to stop himself. About half way through his story, Trallen's mother came to thank him and when he stood up, she hugged him. He was so unaccustomed to such a thing, he did not know what to do, but he lightly held her for a moment as she wiped her tears away. "How is she?"

"Better now that she is home. She wishes to thank you when you are set free." He looked so shocked, Trallen's mother thought it best to explain. "I only meant free of this company. The MacGreagors do no capture."

"I am happy to hear that," Essen breathed. "I cannot be delayed, I must continue my search."

"Search for what?" Glenna asked.

"The golden sword." The whole room went deadly quiet, with goblets touching lips, but tipped no further, smiles fading and eyes cast down. "My father said his father before him saw it. It was held high in the air by a giant."

Patches' heart sank and it took a moment to collect her thoughts, but soon enough her irritation returned. "If indeed there is such a sword, and if you find the one who has it, do you intend to steal it from him?"

The look on Essen's face was one of profound confusion. "I had not thought of that. Father only said that when I find it, I will find my happiness."

She didn't quite believe him and narrowed her eyes. "What do you suppose happiness to be?"

He looked into her eyes for a very long moment. Then he tipped his head a little to one side in defiance. "I have always supposed it to be the love of a very good lass."

Shaw watched Patches look away, knew Essen had gotten the better of her finally, and thought to relieve his sister-in-law's discomfort. "You are right." He reached across the table and took Brenna's hand. "Happiness *is* the love of a good lass."

When the door opened for a second time, everyone turned to see who it was. Carley's husband always seemed late for the evening meal and it was the same this night as well. It happened so often, the family no longer asked for his excuses. Mefrin kissed his wife's cheek, sat down at the table and waited to be served.

Carley was clearly displeased with her husband's embarrassing tardiness and the lack of an apology. Under the table, Patches reached for her sister's hand to comfort her.

"Shall I continue?" asked Essen.

"Oh please do," answered Carley, her happy mood suddenly returning. "You were telling of the MacKinnon lairds who kept killing each other off. Thank the Good Lord we do not have that fret. I can think of no one who is foolish enough to think him capable of winning a battle with my brother. He is a very, very big lad and a skilled warrior."

Essen was about to speak when Patches interrupted him, "But killing a laird is not the only avenue in which a lad might gain the position. He might hope to gain favor through marriage, for example. And there are always injuries or illnesses that cause men to die."

"Are you daft?" Mefrin asked. When everyone stared at him, he clarified his question. "Not Patches, this stranger. We have heard of a daft lad wearing white and wandering the whole of Scotland."

Essen rubbed his brow for a moment. "I believe I am the last to hear that rumor. Indeed, I am daft when it suits me. I was sound asleep when..."

Carley was much better at regaining her happy mood than Patches. Patches only half listened to the rest of Essen's story and the more she thought about her beloved sister's sadness the more she found her brother-in-law intolerable.

Essen noticed the change in the woman he was becoming fond of, and cut his story shorter than he would have otherwise. She seemed reserved, as though she had something else on her mind. He glanced at the last man to join them and wondered if he was the cause. But Mefrin was only interested in his meal.

At the end of the evening, Glenna also hugged and thanked him. Essen was beginning to like being hugged. In his arms, Glenna felt like he imagined his mother would have felt, and he savored the feeling of her soft body and the smell of her clean hair.

Shaw took him to see Trallen and then showed him to a cottage where he could sleep. He was truly exhausted. In the last few days he had felt more emotion than he had in years—from rage, to concern for Trallen, and to what he guessed was the beginning of a strange and wonderful attraction to Patches. Not bothering to undress, he removed his weapons, stretched out on the bed and quickly fell asleep.

JINTY CLIMBED INTO bed next to her twin, pulled the covers up and got comfortable. Old enough now, they lived together in a cottage of their own—at least until one or both of them married.

"So the lad in white has come back," muttered Jinty.

"Aye and Trallen's mother says he is not daft. Never have I known a rumor to be so untrue as that one. Perhaps it was started out of vengeance. It must have been."

"Aye, but we call each other daft all the time."

"But we hardly ever mean it. They that said Essen MacKinnon was daft meant it well enough. Perhaps he is only daft some of the time."

"Sister, you must be right. Does he want a wife, do you think?"

"Well I'd not marry him. Suppose he truly is daft? Marriage to a lad like that could never be promising."

Catella stretched, yawned and moved a little closer to her sister.

"Your feet are cold, move over," Jinty said.

"'Tis because you got all the warm blood and I got all the cold. Mother said so."

"When?"

"I do not recall precisely when, but it is the truth of it. Therefore you must keep my feet warm."

"I suppose it is also why I wake of a morning with no blankets over me. Am I to...?"

"Oh never mind all that, did you hear what Brenna said to her sister?"

Still annoyed, Jinty rolled her eyes. "You know very well I was not close enough to hear. What did she say?"

"She said Brevie's head was bashed."

Jinty caught her breath. "Truly?"

"Aye, she was bashed from behind."

"That is not what we heard at all. Then it must have been a lad who killed her, but which one?"

"I do not know, but would it not be splendid if we discovered him? How proud Justin would be and it might make lads notice us."

"What a fine idea, sister. But what can we do?"

"Each day we shall choose a lad, see where he goes and what he does. There must be something a lad does to give himself away, or a place he goes to contemplate what he has done."

"But the men go into the forest and we are not allowed."

"We are allowed if we are together. We will take our baskets and pretend to look for raspberries."

CHAPTER VIII

ESSEN HAD FORGOTTEN just how good it felt to sleep in a bed. The guest cottage was very comfortable and smelled like lavender. He missed the smell of his mother's lavender spice and wished he could stay in bed all day. Still, he could hear others up and about and he had a sword to find.

He was up just in time. Trallen's mother knocked on the door and when he answered, Blue ran out and she brought in his morning meal complete with warm bread. "My daughter is much improved. Sit and eat while it is fresh." She laid his rabbit fur cloak on the bed, pulled out one of the two chairs, sat down and motioned for him to do the same. Then she uncovered the bread and the bowl of sweet cream. He looked perplexed, so she tore off a small piece of bread, dipped it in the cream and ate it. She watched him do the same and then grinned at the look of delight on his face.

"'Tis honey bread. When we can get the beekeepers to bring us honey, we make honey bread. I have yet to find a lad who does not like it."

First, a woman he fancied, a fitting bed and now a sweet morning meal? Leaving this place was getting harder by the hour. Nevertheless, after Trallen's mother left, he picked up his cloak and started down the path to find Blue and his horse.

He called, but Blue was nowhere to be found and he had no idea where to look. It was not until he reached the courtyard and yelled for

Blue once more that Patches stuck her head out of the second floor window. "He's up here; wait and I will bring him down."

Essen leaned against the short stonewall, crossed his legs and folded his arms. "Traitor," he muttered. "First you prefer Allie and now Patches." Soon the door opened and Blue raced out only to turn around in the middle of the courtyard and head back to Patches.

Patches was not pleased. She had no choice but to take the dog to him and her hair was not yet brushed. Any other time she would not have cared. After all, in a little while she would be bathing in the loch with the women and getting it wet. That thought reminded her to warn him. "The lasses bathe in the morning and the men late of an afternoon. Best not go to the loch until then."

"I do not intend to stay that long."

She should not have been disappointed, but she was. "'Tis a pity my brother has not yet returned. He will want to thank you himself. Where do you think to go?"

"I must continue my search."

She had forgotten about the golden sword. "But what will you do if you do not find it?"

He took a deep breath and slowly let it out. "I do not know." Essen thought he detected a hint of regret in her voice and wondered—if she asked him to stay, would he? He found it very tempting and had to admit postponing his search would not be the end of the world.

"May I?"

It took a moment before he realized what she wanted and held out the cloak so she could touch the fur. "I started sewing it when I was not yet fourteen."

"It is beautiful." Patches did not want him to go, but she wasn't about to ask him to stay.

"What upset you last night?"

"I was not upset."

"You looked upset to me."

He was right and she smiled despite herself. "Perhaps I was a little. I should not say of it, but since you are leaving never to be seen again, and I cannot speak of it to anyone else, I might as well tell you. I fear my sister's husband does not love her."

That would have been Essen's last guess and he found no words of wisdom or comfort to say. "What do you think to do?"

His question surprised her. "I had not thought to do anything. I only just discovered it last night." She realized she was still petting the cloak and stopped. Yet, when he stood up and started to walk down the path toward the horses, she found herself walking with him. "What can I do? It pains me to see my sister so unhappy."

"I know little of such things, but there must be something to relieve her misery. Does she love him?"

"How could she? He is always late, impossible to find when we need him and of little consequence to the rest of the clan." A sudden thought occurred to her. "My brother has given him no important position. My brother knows—he must."

"Knows what?"

"That Mefrin married my sister only to…"

Essen abruptly stopped. Some of the younger men were beginning their warrior practice and he wanted to watch. The longer he watched, the more fascinated he became, and soon he was strolling that direction leaving Patches and Blue behind. This day they were learning how to throw each other down and even the little boys were practicing.

Ginnion, the commander of the warriors, spotted an error, went to two of the smaller boys, showed them where to put their arms around their opponent, and then use a foot to trip them. When he noticed Essen imitating the hold, he smiled and walked to him. "Has no one taught you how to fight?"

Any other man might have been embarrassed, but Essen was not. "I learned by watching the less fortunate fight the MacKinnon lairds."

"If you stay a day or two, I would be pleased to teach you. It is the least I can do, now that you have saved my sister." Ginnion glanced at the hopeful look on Patches' face.

It was only then Essen realized he had left her behind and smiled as she started to come to him. "My dog prefers her more than me. Perhaps I should let them get their fill of each other."

"And perhaps you still have a story or two to tell." Ginnion leaned a little closer. "Our lasses talk of you this morning. Perhaps you might find your happiness here after all."

Essen waited until Patches got closer and then asked, "What do the lasses say about me?"

Patches rolled her eyes. "You'd think we have never seen a stranger before. Come Blue, we are off to do our bathing, but fear not, I will not let the lasses throw you in the loch." The dog seemed to know what she was saying, wagged his tail and fell into step beside her as she walked away.

THE TWINS AND THE OTHER clanswomen were not the only ones gossiping about Essen. Their bathing done and their hair dry, Deora, Glenna and three of the sisters sat in Glenna's sitting room on the second floor of the Keep, talking about the odd reaction Patches had to the stranger. Abruptly, Patches stuck her head in the door, announced Essen was staying a day or two more, and then hurried down the stairs with Blue still at her heels.

Deora kept her voice down just in case. "She may not know it, but our Patches is smitten."

"And he with her," Carley added amid nods from the others.

Ceanna took another stitch in the kilt she was mending for her son. "And since when is Patches fond of dogs?"

"My baby has grown up," Glenna sighed.

"But mother, therein lies the problem," said Ceanna. "We have favored her too much, and she might well frighten the lad away before he is truly in love. She is too bold." Ceanna got no argument from the others.

Matchmaking was Deora's favorite delight. "If only we could keep him here until Justin comes home. My husband would know what to do."

Carley smiled, "Aye, but we told Essen we do not capture, remember?"

Glenna laughed. "How stupid of us." She waited a moment for the giggles to die down. "There must be some way to see they spend time together other than when we take our meals. With all of us together, it is not likely they will talk to each other directly."

"They had no trouble talking to each other directly last night. I believe she was thinking of throttling him," said Deora.

"You were very quiet last night," Glenna said.

"I miss my husband. Besides, I found the lad fascinating. What a story he tells." Deora paused to think for a moment. "Perhaps we might seat him next to her when we take our meals."

"Nay, seat them where they cannot see each other," Carley suggested.

Glenna playfully glared at her daughter. "You are too cruel, Carley. I will seat them much as we were last night, so they can hardly avoid looking at each other."

Normally quiet of late, all were surprised when Brenna spoke up. "I like him, but his clothes are nearly worn out. We cannot send him away in those same clothes now that the clans think him daft. I fear he'll be put upon by others."

"She is right," said Carley.

Brenna bit her lower lip. "My husband could give him new clothing, but will Essen think less of us for suggesting it?"

"He might welcome our interference. Did he not say he had to steal larger clothing as he grew?" asked Glenna. "If we offer, he will not need to steal."

Carley agreed. "Besides, he said he wears the clothing of his banished father, and how long will it be before the clans believe he too has been banished?"

"Aye, a banished lad..." Ceanna suddenly caught her breath. "He said he killed Trallen's husband. If the Kennedys saw him, they might have followed him here."

Glenna took hold of Ceanna's hand. "The Kennedys will not attack; they fear us too much for that."

"Even for a slain Kennedy? We would attack if one of ours was slain, and surely that is what they think."

"We cannot know they saw Essen, and our guards would know if the Kennedys followed," said Glenna.

"Aye, but Brevie was slain and we cannot be certain it was not a Kennedy. Our guards reported seeing no one, but how hard can it be to get close to us?" Brenna suddenly stood up. "I will go to my husband and tell him our concern. If he agrees, I'll see to MacGreagor clothing for Essen. She opened the door and slipped out.

"What if Essen killed Brevie?" Ceanna asked.

Glenna thought about that. "A lad who saves one woman did not likely kill another. Nay, it was not Essen."

"Well, I for one will rest easier when the slayer is caught," said Carley.

Ceanna nodded. "So will I, I hate suspecting every man I see."

Glenna suddenly grinned. "How does a lass know when she loves a lad?"

"That's easy, she misses him," said Carley.

"Aye, after this meal, perhaps we should let Essen and Patches miss each other for a time."

"Are you that certain Essen is the right lad for our Patches? Should she not marry a MacGreagor?"

Glenna nodded. "It is the first time Patches has noticed any lad and I will not have her hurt. Essen is without a clan and he will make a good MacGreagor."

SHE TRIED NOT TO, BUT every once in a while, Patches went to her window and watched Ginnion teaching Essen how to fight. The other men had been dismissed to go to their chores, leaving the two of them alone in that part of the glen. Her attraction to Essen was so unfamiliar, she did not understand it. There was just something about him. He was not more handsome than Donan, but perhaps that didn't matter. Donan never made her feel shy and never had she gone to her window to watch him.

She left the window, sat down at her table and picked up her sewing, in which she had only taken a few stitches since Brevie died. Patches just couldn't seem to concentrate on it and now thoughts of Essen threatened to delay her further. She set her sewing down and walked back to the window. Essen and Ginnion were gone.

"THEY ARE LASSES," SAID Ginnion, stripping off his clothes and wading into the water behind several of the other men who were already bathing. In some ways, Essen was still a little boy and his questions betrayed how little he knew of the world. "Fretting over this or that is what they love."

"Aye, but I ride alone. No matter what colors I wear, I am thought of as banished. I am accustomed to it." He took off his cloths and followed Ginnion into the water. "I do not know how to swim."

Ginnion inwardly smiled. He liked the man and it was yet another reason to keep him here, at least until Justin got back. "It is easy, I will teach you."

"You are a good teacher." He caught the block of soap Ginnion threw to him, submerged and then cleaned his hair and body.

"The lasses also fear that the Kennedys followed you here."

Essen frowned. "'Tis possible, I suppose, though I tried not to let them."

"And there is something our wives have not yet thought of. By now, the Kennedys know both Trallen and her husband are missing. They will soon learn Trallen has come back to us without her husband, and a lad in white brought her here. They will then guess her husband is dead and go looking for a grave."

"Will they think Trallen killed him?"

"'Tis not Trallen I am worried about. If the Kennedys think you killed him, they will lie in wait hoping to capture you when you leave." Ginnion got out of the water and started to dry himself off. "If you wear our colors, perhaps they will think the daft lad in white has moved on. Trallen's mother will want to wash and dry your clothing and perhaps Trallen will be well enough to help."

"I cannot ask them to do that."

"They will demand it and it is not wise to deny a lass such little pleasures." He handed Essen a green MacGreagor shirt and approved when he started to put it on. "When a lass is upset, her lip will quiver or perhaps she will wring her hands. Occasionally she will begin to sob and that, my friend, makes a lad want to kill himself."

"Over as little as washing clothing?"

"Much less occasionally. Lasses cry and lads fight. 'Tis the way of the world."

"Does Patches cry?"

Ginnion sat down on a rock, put on his shoe and began to lace the leather straps up to his knee. His suspicions were right and now he had proof, Essen was smitten with Patches. "All lasses cry, but I confess I have not often seen Patches do it. She is unmarried and 'tis a husband that makes most women cry."

"What does a lad do when a lass cries?"

"I have yet to wholly learn the truth of it, but when Brenna will let me, I hold her and let her cry until she is calm."

Essen's brow was still wrinkled. "And if she will not let you hold her?"

"Then it is best to get out of her way." Ginnion finished dressing, looked at his reflection in the water, took out his dagger and began to trim his beard. Soon Essen was beside him doing the same.

WHEN THEY REACHED THE courtyard, Shaw was standing in the doorway with something obviously on his mind. Essen wanted to check on his horse and was about to leave when Ginnion said, "Remember, you are to take your evening meal in the Keep."

"I remember," Essen said, taking the path down the middle of the glen.

Shaw closed the door behind him and stopped just a few feet away from Ginnion in the courtyard. "Justin has been gone long enough to make it there and back twice over. How long does it take for the king to choose a lad?"

"This long, apparently."

"Our wives think Patches fancies him and they do not want her heart broken," said Shaw, as he watched Essen continue to walk down the glen. "Can you think of a way to keep him from leaving?"

"He wishes to learn how to swim. That should keep him here a day or two more," said Ginnion.

"Good. On the other hand, our wives have not yet considered how Justin might feel if he comes home to find Patches betrothed. He has not yet given his permission for her to take a husband, and you know how protective he is of her."

"Aye, he will have our heads."

Shaw turned his attention to a shepherd in the distance ordering his dogs to move part of his flock up a hillside where the grazing was better. "And our wives will have our heads if Essen leaves."

Ginnion sighed. "Perhaps we could become shepherds. Theirs is a much easier life."

"How would Ceanna like being the wife of a Shepherd?"

Ginnion puffed his cheeks. "She would not like it at all."

"Nor would Brenna. We are cursed, my friend. Our only hope is to let Essen and Patches fall in love, but not let them be alone where he might betroth her."

"How do we do that?"

Shaw reached over and playfully slapped his brother-in-law on the back. "I give you that chore." Smiling, he headed back inside the Keep to continue Justin's daily duties.

Ginnion ran his fingers through his wet hair twice and then headed into the Keep. "And I will happily give it to my wife."

WHEN ESSEN FINALLY came into the great hall, all the others were already seated at the table waiting for him. He quickly found his chair opposite Patches, sat down and looked at her only to find her glaring at him. "What?"

Patches hardly recognized him and with his facial hair shorter, she had to look twice to be sure it was the same man. "Have you become a MacGreagor?"

He glanced down at the green kilt and then looked back at her. "You do not approve, my lady."

Their little war had begun already and the rest of the family could not resist smiling.

"Far be it for me to approve or disapprove. I am just surprised, is all. Green suits you...I suppose."

"Do you intend to keep my dog?" Essen asked, returning her glare.

"He has completely forgotten you."

"Has he? Blue, come." The dog quickly obeyed, came to him long enough to have his head rubbed and then went back to lie down under the table at Patches' feet.

"There, you see, he prefers me," she boasted.

"What spell do you cast on him? Do you tempt him away with affection alone or do you feed him often?"

Patches narrowed her eyes again. "Both."

He couldn't help but smile. "Blue is a good hunter and finds his own food, but I too am guilty of feeding him a hot cake from time to time. Promise you will give him back when I take my leave."

Ginnion quickly spoke up, "Which will not be too soon. Essen wishes to learn how to swim."

Patches ignored Ginnion and pouted. "I promise, but it will break my heart to give Blue back."

"Are there no other dogs for you to love? I have seen several in the glen," said Essen.

Carley giggled, "She does not like dogs."

"She is a thief, then?" Essen asked. "She only prefers dogs that are not hers to love?"

"Might I remind you," Patches started, "It was your dog that preferred me first."

Shaw chuckled. "She has a point."

"Indeed she does," Essen agreed. "But it will break *my* heart if he does not go with me." Essen accepted the platter of roast beef and vegetables, helped himself and held the platter while Glenna filled her plate. He directed his next question to Shaw. "I've been wondering about the clans to the south. How many are there, do you think?"

A second platter on her side of the table had not yet reached Patches. "He chases a silly golden sword still. The lad is daft."

"Dare you call me daft?" Shaw asked. "I too would like to see it."

"And so would I," said Ginnion. "Sadly, no one knows where it is. Be it in the south, the west, the east or the north is any lad's guess."

"Some say the King of Scots has it," Essen said.

Patches rolled her eyes. "Of course he does, the king holds all the gold in Scotland. Everyone knows that."

Essen took a bite of meat, chewed and swallowed. "Then you suggest I see the king and ask him directly?"

Patches flashed a sarcastic grin at him. "I suggest you do whatever pleases you."

She was annoyed with him again and he could not understand why. Nevertheless, he liked seeing her dimples and when she smiled, although it was not a sincere smile, he enjoyed it greatly. "Where do you suppose the king is this time of year?"

"Edinburgh, naturally. 'Tis where my brother has gone."

"Why?"

Patches hadn't even noticed that the others were not joining in their conversation. In fact, she hardly knew they were there. "The king sent for him."

"Why?"

"I am not completely certain. The king asked him to bring five...unmarried..." She abruptly stopped and blinked repeatedly. "Shaw, why did the king want the men to be unmarried? Why would that be a requirement to take a position in the king's guard?"

Shaw hurried to finish the food he had in his mouth, but before he could, Mefrin came in the door, late as usual. He watched Mefrin give his wife a kiss on the cheek, take his seat across the table from her and begin to fill his plate with food. His hair was freshly washed and it was obvious he had recently bathed. "Mefrin, can you not come to the evening meal on time? You begin to annoy us."

Mefrin stopped filling his plate and looked at the all the faces turned his direction. "I do not do it on purpose; surely you do not believe I do."

Shaw decided to ignore the man before he started a fight. Besides, Justin might not approve of Shaw's interference. "As I was about to say, perhaps the king asked for unmarried men so he would not have to house a wife and children."

Patches thought about that. "Perhaps you are right." As it always did, Mefrin's lateness changed everyone's mood, especially hers. She could think of nothing more to say and was grateful when Essen asked again, and Shaw answered his question about the other clans in the area.

DONAN PUT OUT HIS HAND and was glad when Bethal took it. He decided to walk her down a longer path this time just to see, and once they were far enough away, he looked up at the windows of the guard tower. As he suspected, the king was watching them. Donan smiled.

"Have you noticed?" asked Bethal. "Ruskin walks with one of the queen's ladies."

"Does he? I find that very favorable to us."

"How so?"

"I believe he fancied you, but now he has another woman on his mind."

"Aye, but she may not be willing to live somewhere other than here."

"Perhaps the king can find him a position here. If not, a lass must do as her husband says, is that not so?"

Bethal stopped walking and stared into his eyes. "Unless she can convince him otherwise."

He could not hide his grin. "What will she do to convince him?"

She pretended to be completely ignorant on the subject. "I am not at all certain, but the queen will surely explain it. Tell me, why have you not yet married?"

"I did not find a lass who pleased me, so I decided to wait until the younger ones grew up."

"None of them pleased you, not even one?"

Donan thought about it a moment, "Well, there was one, I suppose. Her name was Gretta, she was my same age which was not yet nine and she kicked my shin—twice. It was love at first kick."

She smiled. "I do not recall a lass named Gretta. What became of her?"

"Her mother was English and when her father died, her mother took her to live in England. I wonder of her sometimes. I cannot think it very pleasant to live in England."

"Nor can I." Aside from being physically attracted to the man, she found Donan easy to talk to on any subject and now, on their fourth day together, she was beginning to think too highly of him. It troubled her. Pretending to send him away was becoming unthinkable.

IN THE MORNINGS, GINNION taught Essen to fight and after the noon meal, he taught him how to swim both above and under the water. Essen soon found it to his liking and practiced for hours at a time. However, Ginnion was almost out of things to teach Essen and everyone feared he would soon leave.

Essen found himself in great demand. Beginning with Trallen's family, he was invited to share a meal in a different cottage each noon and evening, at which time he was encouraged to repeat stories about the MacKinnions. He really wanted to be near Patches, but what could he do? Trallen's mother continued to bring morning meals to his cottage and the rest of his time was filled with watching and learning. Ginnion even took him to learn weaving, normally a woman's chore, but it could do no harm for a man alone to know how, just in case.

He was beginning to wonder if he was being kept away from Patches intentionally. He sometimes spotted her walking in the Glen with one or two of her sisters—and his dog. He would have approached them if he could think of something useful to say, but the words would not come. He might have used Blue as an excuse, but that traitorous dog seemed to have forgotten him altogether.

Then one evening he went outside, leaned his back against the side of the cottage and folded his arms. Except for other cottages, there wasn't much to look at, until he spotted Patches watching him from her window on the second floor of the Keep. At first, he tried to pretend he didn't notice her, but each time he glanced that direction, she was still there watching him. At length, he reminded himself he was leaving soon, there was no point in wanting her and went inside.

At mealtime, Patches did not let on that she missed him, but she watched the Keep door often enough to give herself away. Her sisters and mother shared knowing glances, but it wasn't until Glenna began to take pity on Patches that any of them spoke his name. "Essen seems to be enjoying himself."

Ginnion waved his spoon in the air while he swallowed his bite of venison. "He learns quickly and I may soon run out of things to teach him."

Just as Patches feared, it meant Essen would be leaving and it worried her, but she would rather die than let it show. "Truly, a lad who seeks a golden sword cannot stay forever. I wish him much happiness."

"Well I wish him to stay at least until Justin gets back," said Brenna.

Ceanna nodded. "As do I. With Justin here, perhaps we can persuade Essen to tell us more stories."

"Or the old ones again," muttered Patches.

Like everyone else, Shaw ignored his youngest sister-in-law. "My favorite is the one when he pretended to be daft."

Patches got up and went to a small table to pour herself a goblet of water, "Perhaps he was not pretending," she said it so softly they could barely hear her.

"I would ask him to share our evening meal," Ginnion said, "but the other families await his stories and I care not to disappoint them. He tells them quite well."

Patches retook her seat at the table and frowned, "We should have a feast and let him tell everyone at the same time."

Glenna's eyes lit up. "What a splendid idea. As soon as your brother returns, a feast it will be."

"I was jesting, mother."

"Were you?" Glenna held back her grin until she managed to change the subject. "We will most likely be awakened in the night, this night. Mary believes her baby is eager to be born. 'Tis her fourth, and..."

JINTY AND CATELLA WERE again sitting on their favorite rock near the edge of the river. One sighed and then the other did the same, until Jinty finally spoke up, "How are we so easily caught?"

"The men are trained to hear things we do not normally hear. We have followed three men and all three caught us."

"It is because you do not watch where you are going."

Catella rolled her eyes. "Me, why do you always blame me? You are just as clumsy as I am and sometimes you are worse."

"If that be the case, we might as well give up. I had hoped to be more successful, but truly, watching a man stand guard is bothersome at best."

"Then we will never know who killed Brevie."

Catella folded her arms and leaned forward a little. "Perhaps we need only wait until Balloch comes back. He must know something more and I aim to hear it. Besides, we've no idea what it is like to see the King and he will have those stories to tell as well."

"True, how I envy Bethal. She must know absolutely everything about Scotland by now."

"Sister, if one of us marries and not the other, perhaps the other should go into the service of the Queen."

"I had not thought of that. 'Tis a splendid idea," said Jinty.

CHAPTER IX

IT WAS THE DAY BEFORE the MacGreagors were to leave and Bethal found herself more and more pleased to be spending time with Donan. He had many stories to tell and almost always made her laugh. She missed her clan very much and did not notice that none of the stories included Brevie. In return, she told secrets about the castle. "'Tis haunted," she whispered.

"Haunted?" he whispered back.

"Blanka swears it is and has seen the ghost herself. She claims it is the ghost of King William's wife."

"How did she die?"

"Something awful must have happened, but no one knows quite what. I am not altogether sure I believe it, but..."

He was just as enthralled with her story and chose to walk with her down the hill toward the village, stopping often so she would not tire out too easily. As they began to walk back toward the castle, he abruptly took her in his arms and kissed her.

It startled her and she quickly pulled away. "I thought we were just pretending."

He quickly clasped his hands behind his back. "I fully intended it to be nothing more, but..."

"But what?"

"Well, I could say I kissed you just in case the king or Justin was watching, but the truth be told, I wanted to. You are very pleasing and I could not resist."

She hardly knew what to say. She liked his kiss, but was it proper to admit it? Bethal didn't think so, but then, what did she actually know about such things? Suddenly, she could not wait to ask the queen's advice and began to walk a little faster.

Donan caught her arm and stopped her. "Have I upset you?"

"Nay, you have not upset me. It is just that...it was most unexpected."

"Then you did not find it unpleasant?"

She could not help but blush. "It was more pleasant than I care to admit."

"Then perhaps we might try it again."

"Now?"

"Why not now? We have already convinced the king we are set upon each other, and everyone will expect us to be in each other's arms whenever possible."

"But we are just pretending."

He looked deep into her eyes. "Are we?"

Bethal quickly looked away. "What are you saying?"

"I am saying I have fallen in love with you. I did not mean to and charged myself not to, but the heart does not always obey the mind." He quickly wrapped his arms around her again. "Say you will marry me."

She did love him and why not marry him; he was everything she hoped for in a man. "I will marry you." Then his lips were on hers again, her knees went weak and she felt as though her heart might truly stop beating.

JUSTIN WAS NOT ONLY surprised when Donan announced that he and Bethal were betrothed, he was disturbed. Donan was the reluctant one, the man who did not seem delighted with the idea of being in the king's guard. Nevertheless, Justin reasoned even a man of Donan's character does not choose with whom he falls in love. At least the king was delighted and the rest of them could go home in the morning.

"Aye, but I wish my parents to see me wed. Therefore, we will be married..." Bethal tried to say, standing in front of the king's oversized chair.

"Nonsense, my dear," said the king. "You will marry right here and I shall see to the arrangements myself. You'll not be disappointed, I assure you. Let Donan fetch your parents and come back in a month's time. I am certain all can be arranged by then."

The queen shrieked with joy, left her place beside her husband and hugged the woman she called friend, "Oh do say you will marry here, Bethal. I so want to attend your wedding."

It was all arranged and few had anything to say about it once Bethal and Donan agreed. Yet one thing remained undone—Justin still had to tell Bethal about Brevie, and it was a duty he was not looking forward to. He arranged to meet her alone in the queen's sitting room after the evening meal, hugged her when she came through the door and urged her to sit down beside him. Yet, before he could begin, she started talking.

"Are you very upset? You must know I would rather marry at home, but the king is very demanding."

"Nay, I am not upset and I wish you both all the happiness in the world."

"Thank you." She paused just long enough to catch her breath. "I am so happy, Justin. Who would have guessed a lad like Donan would prefer me? He is so handsome and very strong. I thought he preferred Brevie and I know she preferred him. He was so attentive to her when last I saw them together, and I imagined they were married by now."

It was only then that she noticed the stricken look on her laird's face. "What is it? Why are you so solemn, while I am so happy?"

"The news is very bad." He gave her a moment to let his words sink in. "Brevie is no longer with us?"

"She has gone away? Where?"

He reached out and took hold of her hand. "Brevie is dead, Bethal."

Bethal stood up and backed away. "'Tis a cruel jest you play. Brevie cannot be dead; I will not hear this."

He slowly stood up and took a cautious step toward her. "I would give anything to say it is a jest, but it is not." He opened his arms and amid a flood of tears, she rushed into them. He held her for a very long time. She sobbed so hard, he worried she would not recover, but at last, she let go and wiped her tears with the cloth he handed her.

Bethal walked to the window and looked out across the land. "Will you tell her mother how very sorry I am?"

"Of course. Will you be all right?"

She turned and tried to smile. "I fully intend to cry myself to sleep this night, not just for Brevie but because you take the lad I love away with you. I am not certain which hurts my heart more." Justin nodded and was about to leave the room when she said his name. "Justin."

"What is it wee one?"

"When did she die?"

"The week before we came."

"So recently?" She was perplexed suddenly. "Brevie believed Donan would marry her someday. Now I feel shame for loving the lad she so desperately wanted."

"Brevie would never want you to feel shame." Assured she needed to be alone, Justin quietly left the room and closed the door. His question was far more pressing than Bethal's. Was he so shut away from the clan that he did not know Brevie hoped to marry Donan? He couldn't remember seeing them together or he might have guessed. But then, Deora would have said if she saw an attachment between the two.

He walked slowly down the hallway and tried to remember if Donan was as upset at her death as a man in love would be, but then finding her body was upsetting enough. Still, does a lad love one woman one week and another the next?

Justin started down the steps to the great hall and didn't like what he was thinking. Was it possible the man who claimed to find her was also the one who killed her? Donan was certainly strong enough. Still, there were no witnesses and without a confession, how could he be sure who did the killing? Justin was the clan's executioner, but a MacGregor laird does not execute on suspicion alone. Besides, he liked the man and never once saw anything suspicious in his character.

He opened the door to the king's great hall and found it unusually void of people. He was relieved, found a seat at the table, sat down and put his head in his hands. How could he sanction a marriage to their sweet Bethal with such suspicion racing through his mind? At least Donan was going back with him to get Bethal's parents. Hopefully, there was a way to learn the truth before it was too late.

NOT WISHING TO SPEAK with anyone just now, Bethal left the queen's sitting room and made her way up the stairs to the northern most watchtower. A window seat midway up the tower was her favorite place to sit and think. Occasionally, a guard passed, going downstairs or up to the top of the tower, but for the most part she was normally alone.

The door creaked when she opened it and she had already entered before she realized she was not alone. There stood the king with his arms wrapped around a woman. When he heard her enter and turned to see whom it was, Bethal realized the woman in his arms was not the queen.

She covered her mouth, turned and was about to leave when she felt the king take her arm. "Bethal, I..."

Bethal slowly turned to look at him. "I am mortified. The queen will surely die when she hears of this."

"But she will not hear it from you, am I right? I command you to tell no one, especially the queen."

She considered his words and finally took her eyes off his. "None will hear it from me." Bethal looked down at the hold he still had on her arm. "On the morrow, I will be gone home with my laird. You will tell the queen of my love for her."

"I forbid you to go."

She was beginning to fill with anger and having a hard time concealing it. "You can forbid it, but you cannot make me pleasant in your company. What then will the queen do when she sees my displeasure? Is it not better for me to simply be gone?" She started to pull away, but he still had a grip on her arm.

"Is there nothing I can say to make you stay? I am just a lad, Bethal, and..."

"You are *not* just a lad, you are a king. If you commit adultery, then you give your approval for all other lads to do it. How is a lass to trust if she cannot even trust her own king?"

He had been soundly put down and he knew it. Moreover, she left him with no way of defending himself. There was nothing left to do but let go of her arm and watch her close the door behind her.

Her words would replay in his mind for a long time after.

JUST AFTER DAWN, THE horses were waiting in the king's courtyard when Justin and his guard walked through the huge double doors of the castle. What he didn't expect was to find Bethal mounted on one of the king's best mares.

She wore her MacGreagor colors, had her cloth sack tied around her waist and smiled when he noticed her. "I am to go home with you."

Justin frowned. "Has the king approved your departure or are we to be chased?"

Bethal looked up at the tower window where the king stood watching. "He will not chase us."

"You are certain?"

Despite his bad behavior, Bethal was going to miss the king and wished it did not have to be. When she nodded, her nod was more toward the king than to Justin. She waited for the men to mount and turned her horse in behind Justin's, but her heart was hurting. The road down the hill was steep and looking back was impossible, had she a mind to look back. She did not have a mind to.

The king watched until she was out of sight. With her parting words still fresh in his mind, he bowed his head and closed his eyes.

IT WAS CARLEY WHO FELT sorry for Patches so when evening fell, she quietly entered Patches' bedchamber, motioned for her sister to follow and led the way down the stairs. For once the great hall was empty, so they quickly walked across the room and went out the door with Blue right behind them. Once they were outside, Carley looped her arm through her befuddled sister's, and started them down a path between the cottages.

"From whom do we hide?" asked Patches.

"No one, I just wanted to walk and everyone else is busy."

Patches was about to ask where Mefrin was, but thought better of it. It would only upset her sister. When she started to ask another question, Carley hushed her.

As soon as they reached the cottage Essen slept in, Carley walked around to the side and as she hoped, Essen was there. "We came to see if you might walk with us."

"We did?" Patches muttered

Carley gently nudged her sister and continued, "I believe my sister has something to say to you."

Patches wrinkled her forehead. "I do? Like what?"

Carley waited for Essen's nod and then led the way back to the path. "Sister, you have been most unkind to him."

Patches quickly glanced back at Essen. "I have *not* been unkind."

"Ah, but you have," Carley said. "He saved our Trallen and you have called him a name."

"What name?"

"As I recall, you said he was daft."

"Oh that." In silence, Patches walked beside her sister on up the path with Essen following. He was completely void of an opinion on the subject and it irked her. The least he could do was assure her sister he was not offended.

"Go on," Carley demanded. "Tell him you are sorry."

"And if I am *not* sorry?" Just as they entered the glen, Patches stopped, turned and looked at him. "Have you nothing to say?"

Essen raised an eyebrow. "I have come to believe you need no help and especially from me. On the other hand, I forgive you your insult."

"Forgive me?" Then she sarcastically said, "How kind of you."

Carley started to walk again, and was relieved when the two of them resumed their walk, albeit one on each side of her. She was not at all certain Patches would ever speak to him again. "I am pleased that is settled. Essen, from where did you get Blue?"

Essen was happy to tell a different story this time and explained the details. "It took some doing to get Light to let Blue ride atop him, but they have become fast friends." He leaned around Carley to look at Patches. "And I'd not like seeing them separated."

Patches puffed her cheeks. "I promised to let you have him back, did I not?"

"That you did. I was merely reminding you."

"Come with me," Carley said, hurrying them toward the graveyard. When she found the one she was looking for, she stopped. "This is our father, Laird Neil MacGreagor. He died not so very long after Patches was born."

Essen clasped his hands behind his back. "I admit I wondered about your father. How did he die?"

"He caught a fever. It took him quickly and he did not suffer, but he charged his children to heed his words."

"What words?" Patches asked, walking to the logs and sitting down.

Carley followed her sister and took a seat next to her. "He said that the evil among us, even if it be one of his own children, must be driven out of the clan."

Essen sat down on the other side of Carley and to his amazement, Blue sat down beside him instead of Patches. He reached out and stroked the shaggy black and white hair on the dog's head. "I do not understand. Why would he say such a thing?"

"I did not understand either until mother explained it. Our father had a brother who hated everyone, even his own father. In the end, our father had to fight his brother and kill him. Mother said it was a scar on father's heart that never truly healed. Had the brother been banished years before, father would not have been put upon to kill him."

"How dreadful, but sister, why do you tell me this just now?"

Carley put her arm around Patches' shoulders. "I tell you because we never know when death might take us, and it would be a pity to go to the grave having not told Essen you are sorry."

Patches exaggeratedly rolled her eyes, which made Essen laugh. "And is there a lesson for me as well?"

"Possibly, but I cannot think of it just now. I have heard you promised to come back when you have found the golden sword. It is true?"

"Aye, find it or not, I will return. Shaw has offered me a home here if Laird MacGreagor approves."

"He will approve," Carley said. She secretly watched the side of Patches' face. Days before, Carley guessed Patches was being contrary to protect her heart from getting hurt. Now that Essen promised to come back, she hoped Patches would find her relief. Judging from the expression on her sister's face, it was working.

THE EVENING WAS COOL and even with the campfire, Bethal felt chilled. As the days grew longer, it would be a few hours still before darkness enabled them a good night's sleep. She was grateful when Donan wrapped his extra plaid around her shoulders and then went to sit on the other side of the campfire. Justin's sojourners now numbered eight men and one very quiet woman. The evening meal consisted of bread, cheese and meat the king ordered prepared for them. The king even sent two packhorses to insure his Bethal would not go hungry.

However, Bethal had changed. In just a few short hours, she learned her best friend was dead and her other friend, the king, was an adulterer. It was too much. She was quiet because she could not think of what to say. Sitting not far away, she noticed Justin often glancing at her and tried to ease his concern with half a smile. He kept looking at her just the same. Her eyes were still red from her tears and she expected that was what he was staring at. At last, she glared at her laird. "What?"

"You have eaten very little."

"I am not hungry." She glanced at the other men and then rested her eyes on Donan. "Why did you not tell me about Brevie?"

Donan quickly bowed his head. He was unaware that she knew and her question caught him off guard. "Justin asked us not to upset you."

"I see." She only briefly glanced at Justin and caught his nod. "Still, once we were betrothed, did you not think to come tell me before you left? It might have been more kindly said coming from you."

Donan remembered to breathe. "I could not. I feared you would ask too many questions. It was better for Justin to tell you."

"What sort of questions?" She waited, but no one spoke, not even Justin. She had not thought to ask before and now she feared the answer, but she had to know. "How did Brevie die?"

Again, only Donan spoke. "Someone hit her from behind."

"Slain?" Bethal's jaw dropped. "Who has done this?"

"We do not yet know," Donan answered.

"Where did it happen?"

Donan took a deep breath. "She was in the forest not far from the corral when I found her."

Bethal's eyes widened. "You found her?"

Donan glanced at Justin and then turned his attention back to her. "Aye." Her shock was complete and she stared at him so long, he finally said, "These are the very questions I feared you would ask."

She ignored his comment. "I have seen you in the forest with Brevie in that very place. Did you ever ask her to walk with you? She was certain you would. In fact, she thought you were nearly betrothed and that was months ago."

"Bethal, of what do you accuse me?"

She pulled the plaid a little tighter around her shoulders. "I accuse you of nothing. It is odd that she would believe you wanted her with no encouragement from you."

"Brevie was very young. No doubt, she often imagined one man or another wanting her, but I had no such intentions and never gave her cause to think otherwise. If you saw us together in the forest it was because she asked for my help, nothing more."

"Are you quite certain?"

"You do not believe me?"

"Brevie said nothing of other men wanting her. She only spoke of you. You must have said or done *something* to encourage her."

Donan stood up and narrowed his eyes. "I tell you true, I could never hurt Brevie or any other lass. And I say this as well—I cannot marry a lass who supposes I *could*."

"I could hardly marry a lad who loves so easily as you." Furious, Bethal got up and walked away. Her betrothal was off and she was glad of it.

Left sitting by the fire, Justin watched Donan go off in the opposite direction. He was not the only man still sitting who was disturbed by what they heard. He exchanged glances with a couple of them, stood up and went after Bethal. For a while, he just walked beside her in silence.

At last, she spoke, "If you wish to protect me, I remind you the danger is back there."

"You think Donan killed her?"

"Justin, not once did I hear Brevie speak of another lad. She has...had preferred him for as long as I can remember. The clan has few secrets and everyone would know if Brevie was as fanciful as he claims. Donan killed her, I am certain of it."

"We have no proof."

She stopped and stared at him. "You will do nothing?"

"What would you have me do?"

"I would like the lad out of my sight. Can you not at least banish him for lying?"

"'Tis only you who accuses him of lying."

"Well there are others, there must be. I will find him out and then..."

He took hold of her shoulders and waited until she looked up at him. "I will not have you in danger. Word of your suspicions will spread quickly when we get home and perhaps others will tell me what they know, but you are not to inquire. Do you understand or must I command you to stay out of it?"

If she hadn't been so angry, her tears would have clouded her eyes again. But her fury was as complete as any man's. It took a while, but she finally nodded. "I will obey you." When he let go of her shoulders, she began to walk again. "Expect a lass to come to you."

"Why do you say that?"

"I have seen him with another, although I only saw her from behind and I know not who she is."

Again, they walked in silence and again, Justin waited for her to speak. She had a lot on her mind and possibly a lot more than he knew. It was of this he wanted to ask, but was it the right time? He considered it and at length decided it might help if she had someone to confide in. "Why are you here? I mean, why have you left the king to go home with us? Last evening you were happy to stay, but this morning you are just as happy to leave. What has happened?"

"Of that I cannot say."

"Must I command you to tell me?"

"You must not. There are other commands I must obey instead."

She began to walk a little bit faster and he let her put some distance between them. He glanced around to make certain they were safe and looked back at the men, most of whom were watching him. Other commands? Save for the king, there were no other commands that could override his. A sudden sickness began to grow in his stomach and he did not like the feeling. The king commanded her not to tell, which meant there was trouble and the king was well aware of it. Yet why would the king protect a man who hurt her? There could be no other answer. Justin's lovely Bethal had been forced and most likely by the king himself.

There was little he could do but try to comfort her. "You do know," he began, hurrying to catch up with her, "that you are much loved. If there is trouble, you may come to me at any time and I will do what I can to help."

"Can you bring Brevie back?" She stopped, closed her eyes and bowed her head. "Forgive me, that was unkind."

"Is it Brevie that upsets you or is there another cause?"

"Do you mean my short betrothal? I might regret it later, but just now I am too angry." Her lost betrothal wasn't what she wanted to talk about. "Justin, she will not come to you...the lass I saw with Donan, I mean. She must suspect the same as I and she will be too frightened."

"Have you no hint who she is?"

"None."

IT WAS WELL INTO THE night before Justin finally slept. He liked Donan and never before noticed anything uncommon about him, but perhaps there was merit in Bethal's accusations. If there was another lass who also suspected Donan, then how was he to get her to talk to him? Didn't all women know he would protect them? But then, even Bethal's suspicions did not make the man guilty of murder. Suddenly Justin was even more eager to get home.

IT WASN'T EASY, BUT Brenna came up with a way to let Essen and Patches be together yet not alone. One of her husband's favorite things was a flask full of cold water fresh out of the river. It tasted best, she knew, right after a morning of warrior practice. He was expecting her and as soon as he dismissed all the others and was alone with Essen, he was pleased to see his wife and Patches walking toward them right on time.

Ginnion kissed Ceanna on the lips, hugged her, drank from the flask and then wiped the excess moisture off his face with his sleeve. "You are very good to me, my love." He winked at Patches and handed the flask to Essen. "Have I ever told you how my wife convinced me to marry her?"

Essen shook his head and began to drink his fill.

"Oh that old story," Patches scoffed. "Sister kicked him."

Essen finished drinking, handed the flask back and smiled. "Truly?"

"'Tis not the whole story," Ginnion said. "It was at a time when her brother let no man near her. I preferred her for months, but when Justin is riled..."

Patches rolled her eyes. "My brother is not as bad as all that."

Ceanna put her hands on her hips. "Aye, he is and you well know it. He has glared at you often enough."

"Should I fear him then?" asked Essen.

"Aye," said Ginnion. He tied the strings of the flask around his waist and then adjusted it so it rode on his hip properly.

"Nay," Patches said. "You will see, he is a very kind lad."

"So long as you do not cross him," Ginnion added.

Essen wrinkled his brow. "What sort of things upset him?"

"If a lad hurts a lass, he..." Ginnion started.

This time it was Patches, who put her hands on her hips. "Aye, but Essen saved Trallen and Justin will be pleased to hear it."

"True," agreed Ginnion, "but as I was about to explain, there is an edict in our land that..."

Patches didn't want to hear about the edict either. "Mother is planning a feast when my brother returns. The men play games and..."

"And the lasses laugh at us," Ginnion interrupted.

Ceanna put her arms around her husband and whispered, "Games."

It took a moment for Ginnion to realize what she was implying. Finally, it donned on him. "Aye, games." He released his wife and put a hand on Essen's shoulder. "A lad must spend hours practicing if he wishes to win a MacGreagor game. Do you play?"

"The MacKinnons did not play games."

"I see, then you have much to learn." Ginnion started to guide Essen away from the women. "I will teach you and perhaps others will want to practice as well. The first game is with horseshoes."

Essen looked back at Patches and then concentrated on what Ginnion was saying.

Ceanna watched the men walk away and then leaned closer to Patches. "Were you not against a feast?"

"I have changed my mind."

"I am happy to hear that. We grieve for Brevie still and a feast may not be so very merry, but it will be good for us all." She folded her arms and turned to walk her little sister back to the Keep. "Perhaps I should not say of this, but I do not wish you to fret any longer. Our men are worried, they believe you fancy Essen and he fancies you. Therefore, they fear if left alone together he may ask you to marry him."

Patches stopped walking and stared at her sister. "Why do they fear that?"

"Justin has not yet given his permission for you to choose a husband."

"I see, then that is why Essen does not eat with us?"

"Aye, they conspire to keep him elsewhere. I'd not be surprised if Shaw asks the families to invite him to their evening meals. Not that they do not want to hear his stories anyway."

"Does everyone know he is being kept away?"

"Patches, there are few secrets in a clan."

She thought about that for a moment and then another thought occurred to her. She wanted to ask, but wasn't so sure she wanted to hear the answer. Still, if she did not ask now—when? "Sister, before Brevie died she followed me to the loch and we talked of taking husbands. But after, she said there was something she could not forgive me for. I have tried, but I do not remember ever crossing her. Do you know what it was?"

Ceanna lightly bit her lower lip. "It was years ago when you were both quite small. You need not fret over it now."

"Aye, but I do fret. Please say what it was."

"You took her new shoes and threw them in the loch. Do you not remember?"

Patches stared at the ground. "I do remember...now. Brevie said she did not like her shoes and that I always got the better pair. So I...Oh sister, did no one recover them?"

"Only one shoe could be found."

"Did the cobbler not make her another pair?"

"Aye, but it took a week."

"No wonder she hated the sight of me."

"Patches, you were not yet seven. Children do spiteful things to each other. That is how we learn to forgive."

"Only Brevie did not forgive me. She said as much."

"Then I am sorry for Brevie." Ceanna turned them up the path between the cottages. "Tell me, when you are married, which cottage would you prefer to live in?"

"I hardly think it is time to consider that."

"Oh I think you are wrong. I saw the look in Essen's eyes. He prefers you, I am sure of it."

"Perhaps he does, but he prefers the golden sword more." Patches abruptly began to hurry toward the courtyard.

Ceanna watched her go and sighed. "Aye, that is what we all fear."

CHAPTER X

"WHO MIGHT THAT BE?" Essen asked, pointing to the man petting his horse inside the corral.

"Ah 'tis Brevie's father. 'Tis good to see him out."

"Who is Brevie?"

Ginnion suddenly realized the stranger did not know so he explained as they walked that direction.

Essen was horrified. "My mother was naked when I found her, but she had no injuries, save bruises on her neck. It was years before I understood what happened. Was Brevie forced?"

"We do not think so, but we can think of no other reason a lad would kill her." They were close enough to Brevie's father for him to hear so they quieted, took up positions just outside the fence and watched for a while. "'Tis a fine horse," Ginnion said.

Wheelan MacGreagor continued to stroke Light's neck and only slightly acknowledged them with a nod.

"Would you care to ride him?" Essen asked.

"He has no halter," said Wheelan.

"You will not need one. Touch the side of his neck and he will go that direction. Wheelan's eyes seemed to brighten so Essen continued, "His name is Light. When you wish him to halt, simply say 'halt.' He is a gentle horse and will even let Blue ride on him?"

Wheeler looked perplexed. "Blue?"

"His dog," Ginnion answered. "When Essen is in need, he says 'light blue' and both his dog and horse come to him." It was the first smile anyone had seen on Wheeler's face in days. Ginnion opened the gate, went inside the corral, laced his fingers together to make a stirrup for Wheeler's foot and hoisted him up.

Essen held the gate open and closed it as soon as Light and Ginnion were out. Then he smiled when Wheelan touched the left side of Light's neck and the horse went that direction.

"You trained him well," said Ginnion.

"I had years to do it."

"I suppose you did. Justin's father had a horse that astonished us all. His horse would hold perfectly still and let his master sleep."

"That is remarkable. May I ask a question?"

"Of course." Ginnion took two horseshoes and a peg out of a sack tied to the fence, turned and started them toward the middle of the glen.

"Why do you find reasons for me to stay?"

It was not the sort of question Ginnion expected and he was caught without a ready answer. "You saved Trallen and we want you here long enough for Justin to meet you."

"Why did you not just ask me to stay?"

"I see you are not easily fooled. The truth be told, our wives put us up to it. Please do not ask why, I cannot say and I do not wish to lie. Do you forgive me?"

"There is nothing to forgive, I was only curious."

"Then you are happy here?"

"Should I be?"

Ginnion started to chuckle. "I cannot wait for Justin to meet you. You have a sharp wit, Essen MacKinnon, and I find it very pleasing."

AFTER A SECOND DAY of learning how to play the games, Essen went with Ginnion and the other men to bathe in the loch. They were out and dressed just in time. Neither noticed the wind pushing dark clouds across the sky and soon after the first sprinkles fell, the rain became a downpour. Men began to race up the path toward the village and then fan out in all directions. The first bolt of lightning hit near the corral. Frightened stallions began to run in a circle just inside the fence and Ben got there just in time to open the gate and let them out before they trampled each other. Loud thunder rolled through the air, women cried out and children screamed, though the thunder was so loud few could hear them.

Ginnion motioned toward the Keep and as soon as they entered, six men came in right behind them. The women in Justin's family were seated around the table holding the children in their laps.

Patches was no braver than any other woman. Nevertheless, she was determined not to show her fear lest Essen think her timid, and when the wind blew out two wall candles, she took one from the table and went to relight them. She tried not to, but she glanced at Essen twice more and noticed he was watching her.

"Where do they go?" asked Essen, turning his attention to the men disappearing up the stairs.

"Each lad knows his place. When there is lightning, four men go to the windows on the top floor to watch for forest fires. The other two stay halfway up each flight of stairs to pass the word down to us. Then Justin sends lads where they are needed. In this case, it is Shaw who will send them."

"What do the other men do?"

"During storms, the clan is most vulnerable to attack. We double the guard just in case and the lads know to do that. The rest make sure the lasses and children are safely inside and then wait for a whistle."

"What whistle?"

"Pray you do not hear it, for it means there is grave danger."

Essen moved out of the way when Shaw and several other men came in. More lightning lit up the room followed by another loud clap of thunder. He could see Shaw talking to the men, but couldn't hear what he was saying. Ceanna went to the comfort of her husband's arms. Ginnion kissed her forehead, whispered in her ear and then lifted both his small children up off the floor. He told them, Essen guessed, to be brave. Both the little girl and boy nodded and then went with their mother back to the table.

"What can I do to help?" Essen asked.

"You can come with me. We must watch the river for flooding."

Essen glanced at Patches one more time and then followed Ginnion out the door, around the corner of the Keep and down a path. It was the first he'd seen of that part of the village. The cottages were clearly older, although none was so close to the river as to be in danger should the river flood. He watched Ginnion grab a stick and drive it into the ground at the edge of the water. Then both men stood back and watched. In less than five minutes, the edge of the water rose four hands beyond the stick.

Ginnion found two more sticks and measured by putting the toe of one shoe to the heel of his other twice. Then he drove the first stick into the ground, paced it off again and added the other stick. With rainwater dripping off his head, he leaned closer to Essen. "When the water overtakes the last stick, it will be time to move the nearest families and their belongings into the Keep."

Essen nodded. His clothing was drenched, his shoes were muddy and he couldn't remember ever seeing so much rain. At least it was not a cold rain. Water poured off the edges of thatched roofs and joined the streams flowing freely down the paths to the river. And still great torrents of rain fell from the blackened sky. Another bolt of lightning struck a tree on the other side of the river, causing the wood to screech and split down the length of the trunk.

The force of such a thing frightened even him and Ginnion prayed the tree would not break off and fall across the water, causing the river to rise even more. He watched it for several minutes, decided it wasn't going to fall and turned his attention back to the level of the river. The edge of the water was up to his second marker. Other men with the same worry came to watch and be ready if they were needed.

At last, the sky brightened, the lightning and the thunder moved off in the direction of the mountains and everyone began to rest easier. Several of the men tied themselves together with a rope, braved the rushing water and made sure the tree across the river was not on fire. Just in case the roots were smoldering, they drenched it with several buckets of water.

Other men went to find dry clothing and more had to be found for Essen. It was not an easy task since new plaids were always in demand and the weavers could hardly keep up as it was. They might have had a supply on hand, but last year's spring wool was used up long ago. Of all the men, Shaw was the only one in the family who was not wet and went to fetch his extra clothing for Essen.

As soon as Shaw returned, Glenna took Essen upstairs where he could change and hang his wet clothing to dry. When he came down the stairs Glenna sat both him and Ginnion down in chairs near the hearth, so they could clean and dry their shoes. Essen's were nearly worn through on the bottom she noticed, but she said nothing about it.

Serving women were not expected to show up on an evening like this, but Deora thought of that early on. With Glenna's help, she prepared sliced cheese, bread, ripe raspberries, wild mushrooms and hot broth made of finely chopped carrots, peas and dried beef.

"Patches, take this to Essen," Deora said, adding a spoon to a bowl of hot broth. "He is wet through and the broth will keep a fever away." She tried, but she couldn't hide her smile when Patches did as she asked. No one adored matchmaking more than Deora.

Just then Mefrin came in wearing dry clothing; even his hair was dry. Patches handed the bowl to Essen and could not resist. "Where have you been in all our excitement?"

"If you must know, dear sister-in-law, I have been chasing horses." He crossed the room, kissed Carley on the cheek as he always did and sat down at the table. "I am sad to say we could not recover your horse, Essen."

Essen quickly swallowed a spoon full of broth. "He will come when I call him."

Determined not to be depressed by her insolent husband, Carley smiled. "I do hope you have better regulation over your horse than your dog. Blue has not left Patches' side all day."

Essen glanced at Patches, noticed his dog laying down right beside her and tried to look annoyed. "I am quite put out. I fear he is far too partial to lasses."

Standing behind her, Shaw put a hand on his wife's shoulder. "Perhaps we might send Patches out to find your horse in the morning. He may be partial to lasses as well."

"Twould be just my luck." Amid the laughter, Essen grinned and then went back to enjoying the broth. He felt so comfortable with them. It was as though they were becoming the family he never had in only a few short days. It was too good to be true and he reminded himself he could not stay, no matter how much he wanted to. He had not yet found the golden sword.

WHAT WAS ALL THE MUD for if not to build a mud village and two little boys thought it a fine idea, especially since the clouds were gone and it was still light out. They knelt beside the receding river where the mud was more sand than dirt, and began the first wall.

In the mountains, the heavy rain gathered in the streams, the streams rushed into the already overflowing river and when a beaver dam gave way, it became a wall of water.

THE EXCITEMENT WAS over and it was becoming a pleasant evening meal in the Keep until a shrill whistle somewhere outside abruptly brought them all to their feet. Shaw was the first one out, followed by the other men and then the women—all but Patches and Essen.

Essen still sat near the hearth staring first after the others as they filed out and then at Patches. "What does it mean?"

She already had her hands on her stomach as if she was afraid to breathe. "Someone is dying."

Essen quickly stood up, forgot about his shoes and hurried outside barefoot. Other men were running toward the river, but the paths were still slick and one almost fell. Essen turned that direction and followed, but when he arrived, the men were not at the river and several women were huddled together. He saw the other men disappear down the path beside the river and turned to look at two women. The youngest was crying and an older woman was holding her. "What has happened?"

"Two laddies swept down river," the older woman said. "'Tis one of hers."

Essen bowed his head.

There was nothing anyone could do but wait. More women came and all of them kept their eyes on the path, hoping against hope the boys had been saved. Deora went to the mothers and hugged them, as did the rest of Justin's sisters - all except Patches who stood up the path watching Essen.

Essen wanted to help, but he knew not what to do. If the MacGreagor men could not save the boys, what use would a barefoot man who was just learning to swim be?

Just then, Shaw and Ginnion came back up the river path and went to comfort the mothers. "Not yet, but the lads will find them," Shaw said.

THE NEXT MORNING, THE two little boys were still lost and not one member of the clan felt like smiling or even talking. With no recovery, there were no bodies for the families to wash and prepare for burial. There was a glimmer of hope they had somehow survived, but just a glimmer. Justin's family ate their morning meal in silence and although Patches kept looking at the door, Essen did not come in. Even when men came to ask Shaw what needed to be done, they kept their voices low, got their orders and quietly left. When Carley burst into tears, her husband wrapped his arms around her to comfort her. It was a touching scene and Patches was impressed with Mefrin's tenderness. Perhaps she was wrong about him. Perhaps Mefrin simply did not know how to show affection as Shaw and Ginnion did. To comfort herself, Patches leaned down and petted Blue.

Work was the best way to relieve their worry and in springtime, there was plenty to do. Yet warrior practice was set aside so the men could be at hand to comfort crying wives, or to hug their own children and be grateful the river had not also carried them away. Taking long walks was also a way of relieving sorrow and once the paths dried in the sun, many were glad to be outside.

Patches asked Carley to walk with her and with Blue close behind, they started down the path in the middle of the glen. Often, they stepped aside to make room for others coming in the opposite direction. At first, she looked for Essen, but when he was nowhere to be seen, it started to annoy her. Being kept from him was getting old fast.

Carley noticed the look of frustration on her sister's face and smiled. "He can't have left without his dog."

"True, but how much practice does a lad need to play the games?"

"He is most likely off somewhere riding his horse."

Patches brightened up at the thought. "Perhaps I should simply call his horse?"

Carley giggled. "I am tempted to see if that would work." She stopped walking, her smile faded and she pointed down the glen. "Is that not his horse?"

"I believe it is." Patches gave up looking for Essen, took her sister's arm and guided her toward the logs near the edge of the glen. She felt the wood, decided it was dry enough and sat down. "How do you know when you are in love?"

"Sister, Essen may not stay."

"You assume I speak of Essen? Perhaps there is another I fancy."

"I see, well when you are falling in love, it is a joyous time when all things seem new and exciting, especially when you are with him. And when he is not near, it is maddening how you miss the sight of him. You think of him constantly, you remember every word he said, and you smile more often than is necessary. Tell me, who other than Essen has caught your fancy?"

"I confess there is another. Before Justin took him away, I thought I might prefer Donan."

Carley considered that. "Aye, Donan is a very good lad and handsome too. He would fit with our family, although he will not have all of Essen's fine stories to tell. And handsome is not all a man is about. Our Manvil is not a handsome lad at all, but his wife, though she be called bonnie, loves him madly."

Patches giggled. "He brings flowers for her table. I have watched him gather them of an evening and he is very discerning. Occasionally he will toss one or two away if they do not meet with his approval. Does Mefrin bring you flowers?"

Carley's sadness returned, but she tried to hide it for her sister's sake. "At first, but he has cast that aside as I think most men do after a time. 'In love' often fades into 'just love.'"

"I do not understand."

"Well, it is not easy to explain." She looked away and tried to think. "We love Justin and all the men he took with him, and we will be happy to see them come home. That is 'just love.' But if you are excited to see Donan more than the others, that feeling would perhaps be 'in love.'"

"Are you saying we do not stay in love?"

"When you are first in love, you miss him every moment you are not with him, but after you are married, you do not miss him quite so much."

"Because you know he will be with you at night?"

"Aye, and if you do miss him in the day, then you will do the wash and be glad of having something to do."

Patches puffed her cheeks, "So that is why my sisters are happy to do the wash. They miss their husbands."

Carley put her arm around her little sister and hugged her, "Precisely."

"Do you miss not being in love?"

"I miss it very much, but what can I do? We only fall in love once. Therefore, savor every moment of your special time and do not hurry it along. It may never come again."

"Carley, does Mefrin love you?"

"Of course he loves me, I am his wife. What a silly question." She abruptly stood up and resumed her walk. "Shall we go see where lightning struck the ground? I have not seen it yet."

THE HEAVY RAIN ALSO delayed Justin, his men and Bethal. All they could do during the downpour was stay under the limbs of the substantial Scots Pine trees and try to keep dry. Even after it stopped, they traveled at a slower pace in the wet mud and prayed the horses would not lose their footing. Donan and Bethal said nothing more to each other after that first night, and Justin could feel a certain amount of tension among his men where Donan was concerned. It was perhaps unfair. Except for Bethal's accusation, there was no proof Donan had anything to do with Brevie's death. Bethal was upset and understandably so, but a calmer woman might not have made her accusations known to anyone but him. Still, the harm was done and there was nothing Justin could do to change it.

Home, he guessed, was not quite half a day away and if they could go faster, they would not need to sleep on the wet ground. For Bethal's sake that would be a very good thing. Yet there remained the river to cross and they could not know how swollen it was until they got there. Justin often glanced at Bethal and then at the ground. When he decided the path was becoming less slippery, he increased their speed.

For many of the clans, crossing the river at this particular place was preferred. The water pooled in a deep area above and then cascaded down a short incline before continuing. That kept the river fairly shallow just below the incline, at least on a good day. Therefore, Justin was not surprised to see two men on the other side. What did surprise him was that one was Ginnion. He was with another man wearing MacGreagor colors, whom he did not recognize. He nodded and then surveyed the river. It was indeed swollen, but not as badly as he feared. Even so, two men crossed one at a time to test the currents. Deciding it was not too hazardous, Justin took hold of Bethal's reins and led her horse across. Donan fell in close beside her, prepared to catch her if her horse slipped in the water. They all breathed easier once the crossing was successfully completed.

Ginnion had bad news. "Two wee laddies lost in the river yesterday."

Justin's jaw dropped. "Who?"

"'Tis Mark's youngest and Luther, Hugh's middle laddie. It happened last night and we have not yet recovered them. Shaw sent men down both sides of the river at first light this morning."

Not waiting to learn who the stranger was, Justin turned his horse and started down the path toward home. All the other men followed except for Donan who stayed behind and close to Bethal.

Ginnion could not help but notice the tears forming in Bethal's eyes. Most everyone in the clan was related in one way or another and she was his cousin, twice removed. He could not know of her other troubles, but it was easy to see how tired she was. He moved his horse up close to hers and when he opened his arms, she reached for him. He settled her in his lap and tried to comfort her with his warm, strong embrace. "I know a lad who will be very happy to see you." He kissed the top of her head, noticed her clothing were still damp and reached inside his sack for a spare plaid. "'Tis your father who watches the paths. I believe he misses you." Ginnion noticed her attempted smile, unfolded the plaid and wrapped it around her. "Your mother misses you as well, but mothers do not matter, am I right?"

When she shoved her elbow in his stomach, he knew the old Bethal was back and he was glad to see it. He nodded to Donan, waited for him to gather the reins to Bethal's horse and then started them home. "Have you noticed a stranger among us? He is Essen and he comes from the MacKinnons in the north."

Bethal sat up straighter. "But we hear such awful..."

"And Essen says they are all true. We have forgiven him for being born a MacKinnon."

"Is he banished?" she asked.

"Nay," Ginnion answered.

"What then?"

Essen smiled. "'Tis a long story."

She leaned around Ginnion to look at Essen. "I should like to hear this story when we are home," Bethal said.

"And I should like telling it...again."

CLOUDED BY GRAVE CONCERN over the loss of the little boys, everyone was relieved to see Justin and his men ride into the courtyard and dismount. There was something comforting in having their laird back home.

"Ginnion told me about the laddies, any news?" Justin asked Shaw, handing his reins to a boy.

"The men have not yet returned and we have heard nothing."

"Send a lad to find them and report back. We need to know how far they have searched and if we should send more lads. Where are the parents?"

"The fathers are among the searchers, but the wives are inside with Deora." Shaw moved out of Justin's way and followed him to the Keep. "They will be happy to see you are home."

The clan was perplexed to see all five of the unmarried men return. It seemed the king had not chosen one of them to be in his guard after all. They too, were warmly greeted by families who wondered if they would ever see them again. Of course, the most important news—the whispers about Donan—had already begun by the time Justin glanced back.

Once inside and before he went to his wife, Justin held each boy's worried mother and tried to comfort her. There was little he could say, but having him back seemed to help. Then he kissed Deora, put one arm around her and the other arm around his mother. "Are the rest of you well?" he asked.

"Aye, we are all well," Glenna answered.

"Then perhaps you might go tell Bethal's mother we have brought her home. She is with Ginnion and a man I do not recognize."

"That *is* good news," Glenna said, rushing out the door to find Bethal's mother.

Justin's sisters stood waiting for their hug and when he noticed an unfamiliar light in Patches' eyes, he raised an eyebrow.

BOTH OF HER PARENTS stood beside Glenna in the courtyard waiting for Ginnion to bring Bethal home. It was only a few moments more before her father lifted her out of Ginnion's arms, hugged her and then took both his wife and daughter to their cottage. Only briefly did Bethal look at Donan.

For Donan, the reception was one of guarded reserve by the clan, save for Catella and Jinty, who had not yet heard the gossip. Their eyes fluttered, their smiles widened and he politely nodded to both before leading his horse down the path to the pasture. It was time for his mare to rest and graze, and for him to contemplate what was to become of him, now that suspicion was his to bear. He eagerly sought the solitude of his small cottage.

BEFORE HE COULD LEAVE the courtyard even, there were plenty of people willing to tell Balloch the latest gossip. One of the twins let it be known she preferred him, and they waited to see if he could guess which one. He declined to guess, so they told him. It was Catella. There was no mistaking the meaning of the grin that crossed Balloch's face.

That was not the only gossip to be had. It might take days to hear it all, but they could not wait to know all about the sojourner's visit with the king. As soon as Essen left to return Ceanna's horse to the pasture, the subject quickly changed, and the clan began to tell all about the daft man in white—who was not so daft after all.

NEVERTHELESS, INSIDE the Keep gossip would have to wait. For what seemed like hours, the mothers, Justin and his family longed for news of the two missing boys. Emotionally drained, they ate little, sipped on wine to calm their nerves and tried to hold out hope. Yet the passing of time was excruciatingly slow, and the longer they went without any word, the more they believed the news would be bad. Justin was physically tired as well, yet he took time to bathe in the loch and then rushed back, so he would be there should the bodies be found.

While they waited, Ceanna mentioned Essen and his wonderful stories, but even though her brother glanced at her occasionally, Patches was not about to let her attraction to the stranger show. Instead, she pretended to be bored with the subject. Ginnion had come in to be with Brenna, Shaw was waiting with Ceanna and even Mefrin was there with Carley. Essen was not there, no one offered an explanation and Patches dared not ask.

She tried desperately not to care, and thought she was pulling it off successfully, but then something occurred to her—she felt no excitement at the news Donan was home, no excitement at all. She didn't even go outside to welcome him. If what Carley said was true, she was clearly not in love with Donan. Still, was she supposed to feel irritable or even angry because Essen did not come? Was that what being in love felt like? If so, she wasn't sure she wanted it, and why did Justin keep looking at her?

"What?" Patches finally asked her brother.

"You have changed and I wish to know what has changed you."

Patches rolled her eyes, stood up and went to sit by Carley on one of the large, stuffed floor pillows. "I have not changed."

"All other times at my return, you've had plenty to..." Justin began. When the door opened, he stopped.

Out of breath from running up the paths, Tosh burst into the large room. "Both alive!" He bent down to catch his breath, and was nearly run over by the gush of excited people hurrying out the door. Then he stood back up, listened to the shrieks of joy outside for a moment and grinned at Justin. "Bethal is home too."

"I know, I brought her." Justin slapped his old friend on the back and then went to pour him a goblet of wine. "While we are alone, I need you to do something for me. Are you willing?"

He paused a moment more to catch his breath. "I am always willing. What is it?"

"There will soon be trouble and I fear it will fall on Donan. What we must do is..."

"BUT WHAT SHALL WE DO?" asked Jinty.

"I cannot be sure, but something certainly. We cannot remain silent on this subject." Catella pulled a chair away from the small table in their cottage and sat down across from her twin.

"We hardly know anything at all, really. It is not as though we saw something suspicious the day she died."

"True, but we did see him with Brevie often enough and we can attest to him not being with her that day. We must tell Justin."

Jinty rolled her eyes, "And how do we explain why we saw them together so often? We cannot say we watched him, you know."

"But sister, Donan is not a harsh lad. We have never seen him lose his temper, and I for one, do not believe he killed her. Someone must speak out in his favor and it might as well be us. Besides, the whole clan knows we preferred him; it is only natural we would watch him and know who he was with."

"If only we had seen who Brevie *was* with that day."

"Aye, but we did not."

"It is all so perplexing. We like Donan, we always have, but suppose instead of helping him, we cast more doubt on Donan's innocence. We should sleep on it, sister. Perhaps we will see what to do more clearly tomorrow," said Jinty.

"Agreed."

Jinty poured water from the pitcher into her goblet and took a sip. "What an exciting day, sister, and did I not see Balloch look at you more often than me? I believe he has heard the rumor we asked Julie to spread."

"Oh sister, do you think so?" Catella asked. "And is he not more handsome than we remembered?"

"Indeed he is."

Catella giggled. "To think, all our struggles and the way to get a husband might be as simple as starting a rumor."

CHAPTER XI

SUNRISE ILLUMINATED still more spring wildflowers in the meadows and at the foot of the hills. The cows bawled to be milked, chickens pecked at the ground and Justin thought he could see two new colts in the glen.

Before they were married, Justin often stood in his bedchamber window and watched Deora when she walked outside. Now he was doing it again, only this time he watched Bethal and Donan. To be out so early, he guessed neither of them found it easy to sleep, even though they had to be exhausted from the journey. He watched Bethal walk to the logs at the edge of the glen, sit down and stare at nothing at all. From his vantage point, Justin could see Donan in the trees watching her. Neither approached the other and Justin was beginning to feel sorry for them both. Even so, until the killer was caught, there were no words to comfort either of them.

According to his wife, Patches was smitten with Essen and according to Ginnion, the stranger often asked questions about Patches. Deora told of their intrigue keeping the two apart until he returned and gave his permission. She also assured him Essen was the right man for his sister and as soon as he nodded his approval, Deora told Ceanna, who told her sisters, who told their best friends and soon the word began to spread.

Yet when Justin mentioned it to Patches at the noon meal, he witnessed firsthand her contrary behavior. "You are only frightened, it is natural."

"I am *not* frightened; I do not want a husband." She was embarrassed, angry and fretful all at the same time. "I did not know it would be like this. I am to stand in the courtyard and wait to see if any man prefers me? I could not bear it. Suppose none of them ask or one does and I do not like the lad, what then?"

"Then you pleasantly decline."

"Pleasantly? How do I do it pleasantly?"

Deora rarely interfered in any of her husband's conversations, but this was different. "Patches, the men understand. You are young and inexperienced. To say you will not walk with one this night does not mean forever. It means you will consider it and perhaps you will accept him the next night."

"This night? You expect me to...nay, I will not do it. I am not ready!"

Justin reached for her hand to calm her down, "Then that is an end to it. When you *are* ready, you have my permission."

IT WAS GOOD TO KEEP an eye on Donan again for Jinty's sake. Everyone said he preferred and was even betrothed to Bethal, but that was over and Jinty was pleased to hear it. That morning, they decided that talking to Donan first, before they mentioned what they knew to Justin, was the only fair thing to do. So as soon as they bathed, dried their hair, and ate their noon meal they were off to find him.

He was not that hard to find for he was standing guard where he normally did just inside the forest. "We have come to tell you we do not believe them," said Catella.

Donan had been expecting someone to mention the rumor and was not surprised. "What do they say?"

"That you killed Brevie. We do not believe it," Catella answered.

Jinty twisted a lock of unruly hair around one of her fingers, "But did you?"

Catella shoved her sister. "We just told him we do not believe it."

"I know, but..."

Just then, Tosh walked up behind the women. "Perhaps you have not heard?"

The twins quickly turned around. "What?" asked Jinty.

"Justin truly does not believe Donan did it, and those who dare accuse him are to be taken to him directly."

Catella and Jinty exchanged horrified looks. Neither had ever been taken to Justin and everyone said his glare could burn a hole right through a man. What then would happen to a woman?

Jinty swallowed hard. "We did not accuse him, we...I mean. I merely asked him if he did."

Tosh's frown said it all.

They did not want to, and Jinty even thought of running, but they followed Tosh across the glen, down the path, across the courtyard and into the Keep. So upset were they, Tosh had to take each by the arm and haul them forward until they stood before the giant of a man they called their laird.

Justin motioned for all the men to leave and had it not been a serious infraction, he might have laughed at their enormous wide eyes, when they finally dared to look up at him. As soon as the men were gone, Justin nodded to Tosh.

"They were plaguing Donan," Tosh explained.

Justin narrowed his eyes and both women tried to back away, but Tosh was right behind them. "What have you done?"

Catella swallowed hard. "We only went to tell him we did not believe he killed Brevie."

"Why would you say that? Do you know something I have not yet heard?"

Jinty drew in a sharp breath and quickly let it out. "We saw him...or rather we saw Brevie...she..."

"Go on, she what?"

"Brevie was always asking Donan to help her with something. It annoyed him sometimes, but he always did as she asked," Jinty answer.

"He did not ask to walk with her of an evening, and we should know, we..." Catella suddenly felt Jinty's nudge. "'Tis not a secret, sister. We would have seen if Donan preferred Brevie, but he did not."

Justin softened his expression and considered his next question carefully. "Would you say you watched Donan often?"

Catella nodded and Jinty shook her head. "Not *that* often," said Jinty.

"Only when we could," admitted Catella.

"In that case, what other lasses did you see him with?"

Jinty wrinkled her brow. "Other lasses?"

"Aye, surely Donan was put upon to help others."

Catella put her forefinger to the side of her chin and thought about that. "He helped many. There was his mother, his cousins, my cousins, the weavers, the..."

"I see." Justin interrupted. "Did you ever see him take a lass other than Brevie into the forest?"

"Often," Catella answered. "He guarded them while they picked berries, you see. A lad standing guard has little to do, particularly now. Helping a lass is a welcome diversion."

"How do you know that?" Justin asked.

Jinty rolled her eyes, "Aye, sister, how do we know that?"

Catella shot her sister an angry glare, stammered for a moment and then finally came up with an answer, "We are most observant."

It was no secret the twins had been keeping a close eye on one guard or another while he was gone, but Justin let that pass. "Have you said of this to others?"

"We thought to talk to Donan first," Catella answered.

"Good, you are never to speak to anyone about this, do you understand?" As soon as both nodded, he continued, "You may go."

The twins could not get out the door fast enough. They only slightly noticed others in the courtyard as they ran across it, then down the path and into their cottage.

Justin went back to his seat at the table and motioned for Tosh to sit down. "Bethal is wrong."

"Aye, she is. Shall I have a word with her?"

"Nay." Justin picked a ripe raspberry out of the bowl, quickly ate it and offered some to his friend. "She is wrong about his feelings for Brevie, and the twins just said Brevie annoyed Donan. Many a lad loses his temper when a lass plagues him too often."

"That is true, but it does not mean he killed her."

"Aye, but once they get wind of what the twins said, the clan will likely want Donan executed."

"You believe the twins will tell even though they promised not to?" asked Tosh.

"No one is more fond of gossip than the two of them. Aye, they will tell. Perhaps you might have a word with them. Tell them the penalty for telling will be..." He paused trying to think of a fitting punishment.

"Separation," Tosh suggested. "They could not bear that."

"Good idea. Meanwhile, see that Donan is sent to the outer guard positions where he does not have to endure this sort of thing. Perhaps it will be good for Bethal not to see him for a while as well."

Tosh helped himself to a handful of raspberries and stood back up. "Consider it done."

JUSTIN WISHED TO SEE this attachment between his sister and the stranger for himself, so he made sure Shaw asked Essen to join them for the evening meal. Although she was again seated across from him,

Patches hardly looked at Essen. "Tell me, why do they call you daft?" Justin asked Essen when the meal was finished.

Essen washed down his last bite with wine and began, "It was upon a very dark night as I slept. Blue whimpered and when I opened my eyes, five lads stood nearby with their swords drawn. I slowly moved my blankets off and sat up. 'Thank the Good Lord you have come,' said I. 'I feared they might overtake me, being all alone as I am.' 'Who?' The lad directly in front of me asked. 'The dead, is who,' said I. The lad shifted his eyes from side to side and saw no one.

'Where?' He asked. 'Right behind you,' I answered. The lad swiftly turned around, again saw no one and slowly turned back to glare at me. 'Can you not see him?' I asked. 'Tis Laird James MacKinnon.' I looked beyond the lad and said, 'James, tell them how Angus nearly cut off your head."

Essen paused to take a deep breath. "To my relief, the strangers backed away, and even though I begged them to stay to protect me, they hurried off. I shrugged, lay down, pulled my covers up and happily went back to sleep."

Justin laughed. "A fine trick indeed."

"'Twas not my own thinking. I happened upon a lass in the forest who did the same and it frightened me off sufficiently."

"I can see how it would. My wife tells me you have many stories to tell. Might I hear them?"

"Aye, at the feast," Patches said finally.

Essen slightly nodded to Patches as if to say thank you and with Glenna's lively help, the conversation turned to planning the feast, and then to the games they would play. Patches was relieved, and for a moment she wondered how it would be, to be married to a man who was constantly put upon to tell his stories. Then again, it was the same as listening to her mother's stories repeatedly and she never tired of them. Perhaps she would not mind it so very much and perhaps…just perhaps, she would stand in the courtyard that evening just to see if Essen would approach her. What could it hurt to walk with him? She knew him as well as any other man and she trusted him. Yet what could they possibly talk about? She already knew everything about him.

When Justin took his family up to the third floor and the others went outside to watch the courtships, Patches went with them. They were surprised, yet pleased and for her sake, all three of her sisters and her mother stood in the courtyard with her talking, so she would not have to stand alone. To their disappointment, Essen walked away, preferring to go see about his horse instead. He did not come back and after an hour, Patches went back inside the Keep.

The sister's husbands, who until now sat on the wall watching, joined their wives and everyone was disturbed, until Shaw put his arm around Brenna and said, "Has anyone thought to tell Essen how courtships are done?"

Glenna signed. "That must be it."

"Of course it is." Brenna took a forgotten breath. "You must tell him, my love."

"But suppose it is too soon?" Ceanna asked. "Will he think we hurry him to marry her and leave in the night to save himself?"

Each tried to ponder the question, but there was no easy answer. If handled badly, they might just scare him away. "I will ask Justin what to do, he will know," said Ginnion.

There was some good news however. Balloch asked Catella to walk with him. That left Jinty alone, but she was not bothered by it. The idea of going to see the king held her spellbound and if her sister were married, she would not feel bad for leaving her. Indeed, the amount of gossip to be had in the king's court would keep her happy for years...perhaps longer. And if she still preferred a husband, at least now she knew how to get one.

IN HER BEDCHAMBER, Patches went to her window and watched Essen talk to his horse in the far off corral. She was a little disappointed, but not as much as she might have been had she not had something else on her mind. None of the men approached her. How odd. She was certain there would be many, just as Brevie said—many men who wished a position of importance and would marry her to get it—yet there were none.

Patches left the window and picked up her grandmother's hairbrush. Absentmindedly, she studied the carvings in the wooden handle. Everyone knew that Brevie preferred Donan, and Patches thought he was the one Brevie feared would want to marry her. Now he was suspected of worse, and although Patches once thought Donan might be attracted to her, it was clear he loved Bethal instead.

Wasn't that precisely what Brevie was afraid of? That Donan would choose a woman simply to further his position in society? While Patches might help his connections in the clan, Bethal could do far more for him...or at least could, before she left the king and came home.

It still didn't mean Donan killed Brevie...or did it?

IT WAS TIME TO RESUME his search, Essen thought. He loved it here, the cottage the MacGreagors let him sleep in was comfortable, but his favorite thing of an evening was to lean against the outside wall, fold his arms and watch to see if Patches would come to her window. He was getting sick of his storytelling and it was another good reason to leave. Then again, they were having a feast and if he could tell them just one more time, he might never have to do it again.

He'd learned a great deal from the MacGreagors and felt more able to survive in the world than he ever had before, but every time he thought of actually mounting his horse and riding away, his heart began to ache. He looked, but Patches had still not come to her window.

No one mentioned the power a woman had on a man, and perhaps he would have needed to see it to believe it anyway. Days before, he vowed to avoid Patches if he could, hoping to lessen her hold on his heart, but if anything, it made him miss her more. Sharing the evening meal with her family eased him, at least for a little while.

THERE WAS A CUSTOM of bowing to authority in Scotland and when Justin rounded the corner of the cottage, it was Essen's immediate reaction.

Justin nodded, spread his legs apart and clasped his hands behind his back. "My followers are not required to bow save in front of company, but I appreciate being honored. I have come to hear your story."

Essen smiled. "The long or the short one?"

"The one about the golden sword." Justin listened to Essen tell about the little boy and the old man, who he would later learn was his father. It was a very touching story and when it was finished, Justin took a moment to think it through. "I have always believed the love a father has for his son is greater than all others. Your father wished happiness for you, but there is perhaps more to it."

"Such as?"

"Well, he surely knew what kind of men the MacKinnions were. He also knew you would grow up without him to guide you. Therefore, he cautioned you not to learn their ways, and then gave you a dream that would take you far, far away from that clan."

"He would not lie about the golden sword, would he?"

"Were I him, I might have."

"If you had seen the look in his eyes, you would not believe he lied."

"Perhaps he did not then. Still, the last sight of the golden sword was years ago. Who is to say where it is now or if you will ever find it?" Justin watched the younger man glance at Patches' window briefly and then stare at the ground. "And there is another thing. Suppose you find your happiness before you find the sword? Was happiness not what your father wanted for you?" Justin stood back up straight and got ready to leave. "Will you come to the feast tomorrow? I believe you will find it enjoyable."

It meant staying another day and he hesitated for a moment before he gave in. Perhaps he could wait one more day to leave. "I am honored." He almost bowed again, but caught himself in time.

"Good. There is more gossip about the lad in white and it now includes the markings on your horse."

Essen watched Laird MacGreagor walk away, glanced once more at the window still empty of Patches, and then went inside the cottage. He had a lot to think about.

THE NEXT MORNING, DEORA walked to her husband's side in the third story window and welcomed his arm around her. "My heart breaks for Bethal. Is there nothing we can do?"

"I believe you have a suggestion, am I right?" Justin asked.

"Well, perhaps I might tell her Donan has been sent farther away. At least she will not fret over seeing him around every corner."

"Agreed."

"Did you ask Essen to stay?"

"I did."

Deora grinned and kissed his lips. "I am relieved. Have you also told him how to court Patches?"

"That I did not do. I am hoping the subject will come up at the feast, albeit in an off-handed way, so he does not suspect we talk to him directly. I like the lad. Ginnion likes him very much and when has Ginnion ever been wrong?"

"Never." She nuzzled his neck, pulled away and took hold of her eldest daughter's hand. "I've a great deal to do. Try to stay out of the way this time."

Justin picked up their youngest and followed her out the door. "When have I ever been in the way?" he muttered.

THE FEAST WAS ELABORATE, with all in attendance except the guards and Brevie's parents. And, there was plenty to celebrate—Justin was home, two little boys were saved, and none of the men had been chosen to stay in the king's service. Bethal was there, pretending to be happy, even though everyone knew the details of her betrothal, and the setting aside of it only a day later. Donan was not there. Catella and Jinty kept their secret and Justin was pleased with them both. He was also pleased to see Balloch with them; there would be a wedding soon.

The men carried tables and chairs to the courtyard, the women brought bowls and spoons for their families and all savored the smell of a wild boar, killed days earlier and put in the pit to slow cook. The air smelled of fresh baked breads, but the time for eating was not yet. Glenna took the children inside the Keep to tell them the story of the land of Essen, while Essen stood telling the adults his stories outside.

At last, it was time to eat, the priest blessed the meal and somehow, Essen and Patches ended up sitting next to each other.

"How long has Balloch preferred Catella?" Justin asked, seated next to Patches across the long table from Shaw.

Said Shaw, "Twas the first I heard of it when he asked her to walk with him. Do you believe them a good match?"

Justin wrinkled his brow. "Have you an objection?"

"If I did, what would you do?"

Justin took another bite and thought about it while he chewed. "I would try to talk them both out of it."

Essen looked confused. "Are the lasses not chosen and have no say in the matter?"

"In other clans, perhaps," Justin answered. "But MacGreagor lasses are allowed to choose their own husbands."

Sitting next to Shaw, Ginnion chuckled. "In other clans the men just choose, marry and carry a lass off. Here it is far more confusing."

"How so," asked Essen.

Patches listened to her brother explain it, but she was not fooled. When Justin finished, she leaned just a little closer to Essen and half covered her mouth. "They think you prefer me, but do not know what to do," she said, almost too softly for him to hear. "I say we trick them."

"How?" he whispered back.

"Walk with me and I will tell you." She stood up, as did he and together they walked out of the courtyard and into the glen. It was good to smell the fresh air void of pork and bread, now that they'd eaten their fill and for a time, neither of them spoke.

"How shall we trick them?" Essen asked.

Patches smiled. "We are doing it now. We are walking together and perhaps it will be enough to make them stop plotting against us. Never have I known them to be so anxious to marry me off."

"Do you wish to marry? I thought you preferred to stay in your very large bedchamber."

She giggled. "Oh I do, I truly do." She said no more, only because she could not think of something else to say.

"I leave in the morning."

Her heart sank. "But you will come back, you promised."

"Your brother has not yet said I can."

"He likes you, I heard him say so. He would never turn you out."

"Then I will come back."

"I will miss your dog. If I keep him, you would have to come back." He looked stricken and she feared she had said too much. Why should she care if he came back, unless she loved him and what kind of woman would be the first to imply it. Patches looked away and kept right on walking.

Essen looked away too and thought about Justin's words. Perhaps he had found his happiness and shouldn't leave her. But then...

"I am troubled," she said, interrupting his thoughts.

"About what?"

"Brevie told me...she's the lass that was slain last month...anyway, she said a lad might marry me just to improve his position in the clan. I am convinced the lad she spoke of was Donan."

"The one accused of killing her?"

"Aye. Suppose he found out she warned me and it enraged him. Do you think it possible?"

Essen stopped walking and looked back at the courtyard. Someone had started playing a flute and people were dancing. He was worried they were too far away and decided they should go back. "I know so little of such things. What does your brother say?"

"I have not yet told him."

He looked into her eyes for the first time up close and found it unnerving. He wanted to take her in his arms and the urge was overpowering. "We best go back."

He walked far more quickly than before and she hurried to keep up. Had she said something wrong? She couldn't tell and soon they were near the courtyard. He never said another word, but slightly bowed and then left her there.

There was no mistaking the pain in his sister's eyes and Justin was quick to go to her. "Did you argue?"

"Nay," she answered, finding comfort in his arms. "He will take his leave in the morning. You did not tell him he could come back and he goes to find the golden sword." She pulled away and looked up at her brother. "He will not find it and we both know that."

"What would you have me do?"

"Something...anything. How safe can it truly be for a lad alone in Scotland? I fear I will lose him forever."

Justin kissed the top of her head. "I will see to it, go to your rest."

"HOLDING A LIT CANDLE in the dark of night, Justin knocked on Essen's door and was pleased to find the man still dressed. He looked tired and Justin could only imagine the turmoil in Essen's mind. Falling in love makes a man uneasy and Justin remembered the feeling all too well. "I wish to show you something."

Essen nodded and followed him. He was surprised when Justin opened the door of the cottage just across the path. It was dark inside and had obviously been void of people for quite some time. He watched Laird MacGreagor light another candle on the table and a second one on the wall exposing cobwebs in the corners and dust on the floor.

"Hold this," Justin said, handing the first candle to him. He went to the far wall, knelt down and began to remove the first of two stones. "Come closer, I need more light." He waited for Essen to obey, removed the second stone and then reached into the hollow between the inner and outer walls. Carefully, he removed a wide sheath. Then he stood up and walked back to the table.

Essen's mouth dropped as Justin slowly pulled the sword out of the sheath. Instantly, the golden blade caught the light and shimmered. "You have it?"

"Aye, your father saw a giant, a lass, another lad and a laddie. I am that laddie."

Shocked, Essen pulled out a chair and sat down. "Then my father did not lie."

"Nay, he did not. My sister loves you and your happiness is here." Justin waited, but Essen did not speak. "You do not love my sister?" Again, he waited but Essen did not answer. Just as carefully, Justin put the sword back in the sheath, walked to the wall, returned it to its hiding place and put the stones back.

He stood up, brushed the dust off his knees and took a seat opposite Essen at the small table. "When we first came here, the Kennedys thought to take the sword from us. My father was a clever lad who talked Laird Kennedy out of it, but I am not my father. If you say you know where it is, you will likely start a war and many will die."

"You need not fret, I will not betray you."

"I am happy to hear that. Will you also think about what I have said? You are truly welcome to stay and make your home with us. And...you need not marry my sister. In fact, if you do not love her, I prefer you not marry her." There was nothing more to say, so Justin got up, blew out two of the candles, opened the door and followed Essen out. He watched the younger man go into his cottage and close the door. What more could he have said, Justin wondered.

JUST BEFORE DAWN ESSEN put on his rabbit skin cloak, grabbed his sacks, walked out of the cottage and then down the path to the glen. He took Light out of the corral and mounted him. Essen had no provisions, but he could hunt, he yet had one of his mother's golden coins and it would have to do. He had no dog either, but Blue seemed happy here and somehow, the thought of his dog protecting Patches comforted him. He nodded to the guards as he passed, as though it was the most natural thing in the world, but inside his heart was aching. He did love her and he longed to be with her, but it was not to be.

As soon as he reached the narrow end of the glen, he halted and turned around. "Of course," he whispered. This was the very glen his father described and Essen had not recognized it. Now there was no golden sword to find, and that too made him feel empty and alone. At length, he walked his horse out of the glen and disappeared into the forest.

"HE TOOK HIS HORSE?" Justin asked in dismay. "I warned him the rumors included the marking on his horse."

"Aye and he left the MacGreagor clothing behind. He has become the daft lad in white again," said Ginnion, moving a chair away from the table in the great hall and sitting down. "The guard said he left before dawn."

Justin sat down at the head of the table and closed his eyes. "Patches will be beside herself."

"Shall I send men to find him?"

"And do what, force him to come back and marry her?"

"I suppose not."

Justin could feel a headache coming on and rubbed his temples. "I dread telling her."

"Telling who?" Patches scurried down the last of the stairs with Blue right beside her.

Both Justin and Ginnion quickly stood up, but it was Justin who answered. "Essen is gone."

"Oh." She took a deep breath and charged herself not to cry. "The dog wants out." Patches went to the door, opened it and followed Blue into the courtyard. Tears rimmed the bottom of her eyes, but there was no one out and about to see. Perhaps she was not as brave as she thought.

"'TIS THE KING!" SHOUTED a woman. She was nearly out of breath when she opened the door of the Keep—"He has come!"

Justin did not look pleased. The whistle came from the back of the village in the direction of the river and he hoped it was Essen. Instead, it was the one man Justin was not eager to see again.

The King's men rode across the river, up the path and into the throngs of people darting out of their cottages to greet him. As soon as he entered the courtyard and dismounted, the men bowed and the women curtsied. "Greetings MacGreagors."

"Greetings, my king." The clan answered. Their eyes were alight with excitement, boys rushed to take their horses, men welcomed the king's thirty guards and women began to plan a grand feast. No one seemed to notice that Justin was the only one who had not come out to greet the king.

"Where is Bethal? I wish to see her. Bring her to me!" the king shouted as soon as he entered the Keep with two of his guards close behind. "Where is everyone, have you done away with them?"

Justin did not smile. "I wish to speak to you alone."

"Why, what is amiss?"

"I believe you already know, my king. Shall we discuss it in front of your men?"

The king lowered his eyes and with a wave of his hand sent his guards out. As soon as the room was deathly still, he raised his gaze again. "She told you?"

"Nay, she did not tell me. I have been laird for only a few years, but long enough to know the last thing a lass will tell me is that she has been forced."

"Forced? By whom? I will kill the lad myself."

"Then it was not you?"

The king first looked shocked, and then narrowed his eyes and clenched his fists. "What is this you accuse me of?"

"If I am mistaken, then forgive me. But between the time of our merriment that night and the next morning when she took her leave with us, something happened. That very night you claimed life would be too dull to let her go, yet you did not stop her. In the very least, you are privy to what happened and I suspect..."

"Good heavens lad, I laid no hand on her. I could never hurt her, she is like a beloved sister to me and the court sorely misses her. The queen begs me to bring her back." He paused just long enough to catch his breath. "Is she with child?"

"She does not say so. If not you, do you know who has done this? I should like to help you kill him."

"She was not forced, not to my knowledge." The king released his clenched fists, took his red cloak off and laid it across the back of a chair. "She is young in the ways of lads and lasses, and she dearly loves the queen. Bethal happened upon me when I was kissing a lass not my wife." He turned, took a few steps away and then turned back. "I shall never forget her words: she asked how she was to trust a lad when she could not trust her own king."

"And that is all?"

"All that I am aware of. I came to ask her to forgive me and go back with me."

It was not such a bad idea, Justin thought. Bethal was miserable at home and time away might be just what she needed. He was about to agree when Bethal walked in.

Her eyes instantly lit up. She walked to him and then curtsied to her king. "I am happy to see you."

"Is that all I get. As I recall, when you greeted your laird you flew into his arms."

She grinned. "Aye, but he wears no crown I might dislodge."

How he had missed her grin and her banter. He lifted his crown off his head and handed it to Justin. "There, say I am forgiven and then welcome your old friend properly."

Bethal went into his arms, let him hug her and then stood back. "I admit I missed you, but forgiving you is another matter altogether. Have you given up your wondering eye?"

"I assure you, you will never again find me in such circumstances."

Bethal turned to smile at Justin. "He means he has found a place I cannot discover him, but I will pretend he has given it up."

"Then you will come home with me?" asked the king.

"I would like that very much. Do you still promise I can come home to visit twice a year?"

"Of course I do. Now, when shall the wedding be? I have thought of little else. We've not had a splendid wedding since my..." The look on her face cautioned him to stop. "What has happened?"

It was Justin who answered, "Bethal is convinced Donan killed Brevie."

"Have you any proof?"

Again it was Justin who answered, "Nay and if he has been falsely accused, then I am ashamed of us all. The clan shuns the lad and I have been forced to appoint him guard duty some distance away."

The king paused to rub his brow. "Yet he stays?"

"He professes innocence and says going would only confirm their suspicions. His words are wisely spoken and I tend to doubt he is guilty."

"I do not doubt it," muttered Bethal.

"No wedding plans then. But perhaps the villagers near the castle might have a festival. I've not been to one in years. Now, my dear go fetch your parents. I should like to meet the ones who grew up such a pleasing lass."

CHAPTER XII

THE KING WAS GONE, taking Bethal with him, but it was Essen Justin was most worried about. The first night, he checked and the golden sword was still there. At least the man his sister loved was not a thief. Patches was right, however, Essen was not safe in the world alone. In the next three days, there was no word of him and surely gossip of the daft man in white would come their way quickly. The lack of gossip worried Justin most. Had the Kennedy's lay in wait for him to leave, as Ginnion feared they might?

It was one of those rare times when Justin went to sit beside the river and listen to the water rushing toward the sea. Patches was being very brave, but there was pain in her eyes. Carley seemed to be taking it just as badly, but then she and Patches had always been close. Even the dog looked bewildered, tipping his head to one side and then the other. Once more, he wondered if Ginnion was right. He should have gone after Essen for the sake of his sister. But then what?

Justin abruptly stood up and whistled for his men. He might fail to bring Essen back, but at least he would know he tried. In less than two hours, he and six others collected provisions, mounted and rode out to find Essen. Justin took Blue with him. If anyone could find the man, his dog could, and by the time they reached the end of the glen, Blue had taken the lead.

IT WAS ALMOST DARK and Justin was about to call a halt when Blue barked and raced into the trees. A few minutes later, they found Essen sitting beside a pond with the dog licking his face and nearly pushing him over.

"So, you are not a traitor after all," said Essen. It was then he heard the horses, got to his feet and turned around. "Laird MacGreagor?"

Justin slid down off his horse and nodded his greeting. "We thought you might be hungry. We brought food."

"I am indeed. I've not had much good fortune hunting. It seems Blue is the one who most often finds our food." He nodded to the other men as they dismounted and watched as two of them unpacked, cheese, apples and loaves of bread. "I do not recall ever being so hungry. Thank you."

Justin nodded. He crossed his feet at the ankles and sat down across from Essen on the grass. Then he waited for Essen to finish his meal and nodded for the other men to move away. A full moon glistened across the pond and the air was warm and calm when Justin said, "You did not answer my question."

"What question?"

"Do you love Patches?"

"'Twould do no good if I did."

"Why not? She thinks I have frightened you away. Have I?"

"Nay, 'tis not you who frightens me."

"Who then?"

Essen stared at the edge of the water trying to find the right words. "When I was not yet twelve, my mother was slain."

"I know and I am sorry for your pain."

"All those years, I did not know how angered I was by it. When I discovered Trallen's husband hurting her, I...I did not just kill him, I slaughtered him. I did not even allow him to draw his sword."

"I see."

"Do you? I do not see at all. Until that moment I had never known rage and I tell you true, I do not know how to prevent it from happening again."

"You are afraid you will hurt Patches," said Justin.

"I do not want to hurt her; I would rather die than ever cause her harm, but what if I cannot prevent myself?"

"Well, if you hurt her, I would have to kill you."

"I find no humor in that, MacGreagor."

"It is not a laughing matter. In our clan, the laird is duty bound to kill any lad who hurts a lass or a child. It is an edict handed down through many generations. I would not like to do it, but I *would* kill you."

"In a fair fight?"

"Nay, when a lass is harmed, she is not given weapons to defend herself. So it will be for the lad who harms her. You will be held down and I will drive my sword through your heart."

"You would be enraged enough to do that."

"Patches is my sister and I would certainly be enraged enough, but I must wait until my rage has passed. I must be certain my mind is clear and I do not kill out of anger." He waited for Essen's response, and when there was none, he continued, "Such a time also allows the guilty to consider his crime and make his peace with God."

Again, Essen said nothing. He was indeed a troubled man but Justin was impressed. Only a good man would be worried about hurting his wife. "Essen, you are not the first to lose control, nor will you be the last. MacGreagor men lose their tempers as often as other men, but they have learned to leave their homes until they have calmed down. Our women understand this too—at least most do. Some lasses do not care to understand much of anything, it seems."

"Is Patches very upset?" Essen asked.

"She cries, but she does not let me see."

"Will she forgive me for leaving?"

"Tell her why and she will forgive you."

"But then she will fear me."

"Perhaps, but the truth is better than to let her think you've run off to be in the bed of some other lass. That, she would not forgive, nor would I."

"Does she think that?"

"If not yet, she will soon enough. It is how the mind of a lass works and you have given her ample time to think the worst. If I were you, I would make haste your return."

Essen finally remembered to breathe deeply. "I know nothing of having a wife. What does a lad do?"

Justin tried not to, but he began to laugh and called his men back. He nodded for two to stand guard, motioned for the others to sit and repeated Essen's question. By the time he lay down to sleep, Essen had more advice than he knew what to do with.

The next morning, after they finished their meal and were about to collect their horses, one of the MacGreagors softly whistled and twenty-five Kennedys stepped out of the trees with swords drawn. They wore red kilts with a patch of matching cloth over their right shoulders.

Ginnion moaned. "I have eaten too much, I am seeing red."

"So am I," muttered Justin.

Laird Kennedy smirked. "We want the lad in white and that is all, MacGreagor. He killed one of ours."

"Aye," Justin said. "And I regret he did not save the killing for me. Your lad beat his MacGreagor wife."

Laird Kennedy watched all of the MacGreagor men nod their agreement and then turned his attention back to Justin. "The penalty for hurting a lass is a MacGreagor decree, but we do not live by it. Yet the penalty for killing a Kennedy warrior is death and you well know it, MacGreagor."

Justin rolled his eyes, "Aye, but we will not give him up. He is daft, you see. Do Kennedys kill the daft?"

Essen began to wring his hands and pout. "I are not..."

"Silence," Justin harshly said.

For a long moment, Laird Kennedy sized Essen up. It appeared the man was on the verge of tears. "Daft or not, give him over and I will decide what to do with him."

Justin glared. "We will not give him over. If you want him, you will have to kill me to get him. Is a war with the MacGreagors truly what you want?"

Laird Kennedy looked at the very large MacGreagor men and then at his much smaller Kennedys. "'Tis your final word?"

"Aye." Justin quickly realized he had not given his opponent any way to save face and tried to think of something. "Perhaps a different penalty will do. A daft lad cannot be held accountable. It is unseemly; all of Scotland will hear of it and think you unkind."

"What do you suggest, then?"

"A flogging," one of the Kennedy warriors said.

Justin was horrified. "A flogging? And if his wounds do not heal and he dies, it would be the same as killing him—only a much slower and far more painful death."

"Refuse to let him marry," Ginnion suggested.

Justin turned to look at his brother-in-law. It took a moment for him to see the wisdom in Ginnion's words. "But he begs to marry right away."

"He *did* kill a lad; he deserves some punishment," Ginnion reminded him.

Laird Kennedy was not convinced. "You would let a lass marry a lad who is clearly daft?"

Justin took a step closer to his opponent and bowed his head. "She is daft too."

Laird Kennedy's eyes brightened. "Is she?"

"Aye. Say the truth of it; is not marriage to a daft lass enough punishment for any lad?"

"A lifetime of misery? You have a point, MacGreagor." Laird Kennedy finally put his sword back in its sheath. "Will you say I was kindly toward him?"

"I will indeed. You are a very good lad, Kennedy, and I shall remember it." Justin returned his opponents nod, watched the Kennedys retreat and remembered to breathe.

SHE HAD BEEN AT THE window for hours, it seemed and when at last she spotted her brother and Essen, Patches was thrilled. That evening, she was happy to stand in the courtyard with the other unmarried women and as she hoped, Essen came to ask her to walk with him. He was once more dressed in MacGreagor clothing and to her, he was as handsome as ever.

He explained, as best he could, why he left and watched to see her reaction. Though she said nothing, she seemed to accept it with grace and he was relieved.

Patches already knew, Justin told her. Besides, she was far more intrigued with the light in his eyes. He seemed to have something else he wanted to say, but couldn't quite get it out, so they just walked together for a time.

Finally, he stopped and took her hand. "I know not how to say it, so I will simply say it. Would you be willing to give up your grand bedchamber to come live with me in a small cottage?"

Patches grinned. "Do you mean you are willing to suffer the misery of marriage to a lass who is clearly daft?"

He chuckled. "Your brother worried that rumor might get to you before he could explain."

"It nearly did. Jinty was about to tell me when I went to the courtyard to..."

"Patches, I can wait no more. Will you marry me?"

"I can think of nothing I desire more." When he did not take her in his arms, she moved to stand in front of him and put her hand on his chest. "I believe you are to kiss me now."

"I have never..." Before he could continue, she was in his arms and when he lowered his lips to hers, remembering how the men said it was done, he found in her kiss the happiness his father found with his mother.

THE OUTSIDE WEDDING was a grand affair with tables heavy laden with every kind of good food and delight, set out in front of the Keep. A few weddings ago, someone fashioned a flower trellis under which the happy couple could stand, while the priest commenced the vows he had long ago committed to memory. Justin put his arm around Deora, Ginnion smiled at Ceanna, Shaw held Brenna's hand and Glenna grinned from ear to ear, as the long-winded priest said all the right words. Even Mefrin seemed happy to have Carley by his side and he too put an arm around his wife.

Everyone was there, even Brevie's parents—except for Donan who preferred to remain at his post and watch for Kennedys. It wasn't likely Laird Kennedy believed Justin's own sister was daft, would soon hear of the wedding and know he'd been had. Still, there was no sight of them, or any rumors they planned to attack. And there would be if that were the case—an impending war was never a secret for long in Scotland.

When it was time and the merriment was over, Essen took Patches to their cottage, opened the door, followed her inside and closed the door behind him. A few minutes later, the light inside the cottage went out.

TWO WEEKS PASSED AND the MacGreagors settled into their usual routine of tending chores, raising children and gossiping. It was nearly time for the evening meal when Lonie burst into the great hall. Every head turned and the look on his face betrayed his anger. "I seek to set aside my wife."

"What?" Justin asked. Such a thing had happened in the past, but not often and never while Justin was laird. "Why?"

"She beds another."

"Are you certain?"

"Come see for yourself." Lonie opened the door and led the way. He ran out of the courtyard, down the path between the cottages and headed into the forest.

Right behind him, Justin, Ginnion and Shaw followed. Justin had a sick feeling in his stomach. He knew, or at least suspected whom he would find with Lonie's wife and he was not eager to see it. He caught up with the man, grabbed his arm and motioned for him and the others to stay back. Then he quietly walked into the forest. He could hear them before he could see them and when he discovered where they were, he spread his legs apart, crossed his arms and loudly cleared his throat.

So alarmed was Mefrin, he instantly rolled off her and tried to sit up, while she scooted away and covered herself. His eyes were wild at first, but when he realized it was Justin, his expression turned to defiance. "Will you break your sister's heart? She loves me and she will surely suffer if she knows."

"I will not have to tell her. Walk into the glen if you dare, half the clan will be there waiting to see who beds Lonie's wife. Carley will know everything soon enough."

"Aye, but she will forgive me."

"Perhaps, but I will not." He walked to the woman, gave her his hand and helped her up. "Your husband is asking to set you aside and I am inclined to petition the Pope on his behalf. What..."

She tightly grabbed hold of Justin's arm as though she meant to hide behind him. "Mefrin killed Brevie. I saw him do it and he said if I did not bed him, he would kill me too."

Justin's glare was hot when he moved the woman behind him and began to draw his sword. "Get up, Mefrin; you know the punishment for murder." When Mefrin did not move, Justin's rage increased. He shouted for his guard and then gritted his teeth. "Have you the courage to get up or is your only valor that of preying on helpless women?"

"But think of Carley," Mefrin tried again, his defiance yet remaining in his expression.

A moment later, Lonie, Shaw and Ginnion arrived, followed by two others. "He killed Brevie and Marion was witness to it. Take him to the storehouse." Justin watched Ginnion and Shaw stand the man up and hardly noticed the other two men quickly leaving. "I will see to his execution in the night." Then he glared at Mefrin once more. "Carley will survive these troubles; you will not!" With that, he turned and walked back out of the forest.

This day came to all MacGreagor lairds and it was foolish to think Justin would never have to face it. For the death of Brevie, however, he had no qualms. First, he had to find Carley before someone else told her. He went to the Keep but Carley had gone to her cottage.

At the soft knock on her door, Carley was surprised to find Justin there. "Brother, I cannot remember the last time you came to see me."

"Then you have not yet heard?" He walked inside and closed the door behind him.

It was only then she noticed the disturbed look on his face. "What has happened?"

He opened his arms and when she went into them, he held her close for a long moment. "Mefrin killed Brevie. Marion saw him do it."

She leaned back to see the truth in his eyes and then pulled completely out of his arms. Carley could not find any words to say and in her shock, went back to cutting slices of cheese at the table. Then a single tear rolled down her cheek.

Justin walked to the pitcher on her shelf and poured her a goblet of wine. He held it out to her, waited for her to lay her knife down and then helped her drink. Her hands were shaking and he was certain she would soon collapse...but the words he spoke next had to be said, "You know what I must do and I pray you will not hate me for it."

She took hold of the back of a chair, pulled it out and sat down. "I have loved you far longer than I loved him. His love for me was false from the very beginning."

"I know." Justin sat down in a chair on the other side of the small table and took her hand. "There is more. He forced Marion to..."

"Do not say it." She wiped her single tear with her hand and closed her eyes. "I once followed him; he has been bedding her for months."

"And you did not come to me?"

"What could you have done? Even you cannot make a lad love his wife."

Justin put his other hand over hers. "Marion's husband took me to see for myself."

"The poor lad suspected weeks ago. I once saw him looking at me with pity and his meaning was clear. When will you do it?"

She was too calm and it greatly concerned him. "In the night."

"Mefrin is not a brave lad. Take him far away where I cannot hear him cry out or worse, beg for mercy." She pulled her hand out of his and put them both in her lap. "Oh Justin, how shall I ever face Brevie's parents. I am to blame. I should have let his treachery be known. If I had..."

"You are not to blame; you did not know he would kill someone."

"I thought only of my own misery. What is to become of Marion?"

"Her husband must decide."

"See that she is not shunned. Mefrin can be very charming when he wants something."

Justin watched her bite her lip and cast her eyes down. He expected more tears and waited for them, but her cheeks remained dry, and he wondered if she was holding them back for his sake. Nothing in the things his father taught him prepared him for a moment such as this. He was put upon to execute his own sister's husband and it mortified him.

"Sister, I must know...are you with child?"

She found his question surprising, although perhaps she should not have. Her mother and two of her sisters had asked the same recently. "Nay, there will be no issue from this marriage." She looked up at the ceiling for a moment. "I cannot even recall the last time he desired me."

"Come to the Keep. Mother will want to..."

"Not yet." Carley stood up, went to the door and opened it wide. Then she went to the bed, pulled the bedding off and threw it out the door. Next, she pulled down Mefrin's shield, tossed it out and went for the extra clothing he had hanging on a hook. "I've a cottage to clean."

Mindful not to get hit with something, Glenna peeked around the edge of the doorway. "You have told her?"

"Aye." Justin stood up, waited until Carley finished throwing the clothing out and then quickly slipped out the door. He had only just gotten out of the way when Carley threw her husband's goblet and bowl outside.

STRIPPED OF HIS WEAPONS and being escorted across the glen to the MacGreagor storehouse, Mefrin was shocked when he felt a sword enter his back and come out through his stomach. He stopped, looked down in disbelief and then sunk to his knees. The man behind him put a foot to his back, shoved Mefrin face down and pulled his sword back out. The man's rage was so complete, he thought to cut off Mefrin's head as well, but then he felt a hand on his arm.

Ginnion was just strong enough to keep Brevie's father from raising his sword and doing the final deed. "He deserves to suffer."

It took a moment, but once the words sunk in, Brevie's father nodded. With dozens watching, Mefrin began to whimper and slowly crawl toward the Keep, as though he thought someone there would help him. His blood soaked into the ground and left a path behind him. With each movement, he grew weaker until at last, he collapsed on the ground.

"May the evil die with you," Brevie's father muttered. He wiped his sword clean with a cloth, put it back in its sheath and tossed the cloth on Mefrin's back. Then he walked toward his cottage to tell his wife what he had done. Brevie was their only child.

Too ashamed to claim him, his relatives did not wash Mefrin's body. He was merely put in a box and once the lid was nailed shut with wooden pegs, six men carried him away while others brought buckets of water to wash the blood into the ground. There was no MacGreagor plaid draped over his box, nor was he buried in the graveyard where the honored rested. Instead, he was taken to a little known place where two other men, who once tried to burn a woman alive, were buried.

Glenna talked Carley into staying in Patches' old bedchamber where she would not have to be alone with her suffering.

Justin was relieved he didn't have to carry out the execution, but there was yet one more thing to set right. He chose the same guards he took to find Essen, mounted his horse and set out to find Donan. It took time, but Justin kept whistling until he finally managed to find him in the forest.

Donan was finished with his noon meal and was about to call his horse when he heard the whistles, returned with one of his own and waited. He was surprised as well as disturbed when Justin dismounted. "What is it, what is wrong?"

"Do you still love Bethal?"

"Please say nothing has happened to her."

Justin smiled. "Then you do still love her. Gather your things, you must take your leave soon." Donan just stood there staring at Justin. "Mefrin killed Brevie and we have a witness. Bethal has gone with the king and 'tis time to go after her. What say you?"

He did not answer. Instead, he kicked dirt on what was left of his fire, gathered his things and called his horse. In the blink of an eye, he was mounted and hurrying away.

Justin laughed and then looked at Ruskin. "Are you not going with him? I have heard you prefer one of the queen's maids and a MacGreagor should not go off alone."

Ruskin was thrilled, turned his horse and hurried away.

IT WAS NOT EASY CATCHING up with Donan, the man rode as though his kilt was on fire. Finally, Ruskin managed it, encouraged Donan to slow down for the sake of the horse and even got him to rest occasionally. It took most of three days to cover the distance between the MacGreagor hold and the king's castle, and once there, Ruskin had to remind Donan to bathe first. It was all becoming laughable and Ruskin was enjoying himself thoroughly. Then it occurred to him, he too had to convince a woman to marry him, and he was not at all certain he knew the right words.

Therefore, two MacGreagor men stood in line before the king in the great hall and waited their turn to have a say. Messengers came and went, commanders got the king's attention immediately and Donan started to get anxious. Suppose Bethal still rejected him? Nothing in his entire life frightened him more. He tried not to think of how she felt in his arms, or the warmth and passion in her kisses.

Suddenly, Bethal was standing before him, holding a tray of sweet breads for the king to taste. "Why have you come?"

He could hardly speak. She was even more beautiful than he remembered and with her standing so close to him, he feared his heart would stop beating.

Ruskin took pity, "Bethal, Mefrin killed Brevie, not Donan."

Her eyes widened. "Truly?"

"Truly, Marion saw Mefrin do it."

"Mefrin? Did he hurt Carley?" she asked.

"Nay," Donan finally managed to say. "She is well, although shamed by her husband's evil."

When the king walked up behind her the others quieted, but Bethal did not notice. "I would be too." She closed her eyes for a moment and blinked back her tears. "I too am shamed, for I accused you falsely. Can you ever forgive me?"

"Only if you agree to marry me. I love you, Bethal. I love you more than life."

The king's eyes brightened and his smile was wide. "A wedding after all? How delightful. Will you stay, lad, or do you intend to carry Bethal away with you?"

"I leave it up to her to choose, my king." He remembered to bow and then winked at her.

"Well now, let me see." Bethal lightly kissed Donan on the cheek and then walked completely around the king. "I wish to see my family more than twice a year. Aye, three or four times at least. And then there are the living arrangements." She continued to make a circle around the king wider each time with the people moving back so she could. "We wish a cottage of our own, not so very far away from the queen, mind you, and I desire a horse to bring me here when I am invited. Your hill is murderous to climb, you understand. I will also need a Slype-Groat board of my own to practice on, now that you have become more proficient than I, and..."

~The End~

Abducted

Book 8

Marti Talbott's Highlander Series
Sample chapter

Born the second child of Laird Justin MacGreagor, Paisley was a rare blue-eyed beauty with hair that turned snowy white before she reached her sixteenth birthday. Once rumors spread of her beauty, unmarried men from miles around came just to see her.

Laird Chisholm Graham only spent a few hours with Paisley, but it was enough to know he wanted to make her his wife. Yet, as desperate as her father was to protect her, it was not enough to keep her from being abducted. Who took her and how were they ever going to get her back?

CHAPTER I

IT WAS ABOUT THIS CHILD Laird Justin MacGreagor worried most. She had his determination and her mother's defined features, but Paisley had something more than most women. Born second eldest, her long hair went from pale yellow to white by the time she reached the age of sixteen. Her hair made her blue eyes mesmerizing and warriors, young and old alike, could not seem to keep from gawking at her. The moment she entered the great hall, a laird's place of constant clan business, the men quieted just to watch her—a habit Justin found extremely irritating. His daughter liked it even less and often glared at the men or crossed her eyes.

One day two MacDuff brothers mentioned her extraordinary beauty to another man in a marketplace, who told another and another. Word began to spread all across Scotland and Justin MacGreagor's nightmare had only just begun.

FOR THE MOST PART, life in the MacGreagor clan was pleasant. The forests surrounding their glen offered sufficient hunting and the river behind the village held an abundance of fish. Flocks of sheep supplied mutton for food and wool for their clothing, cows gave them milk and farmers raised vegetables in the adjoining valley. Always there were birds chirping in the trees and the sweet smell of Scots Pine in the forest filled the air when the breeze blew just right.

Old and new cottages bordered meandering paths that met in the wide courtyard in front of the Keep. Two halves of a short stonewall bordered the courtyard and offered a place to sit in the sunshine Scotland normally saw too little of. The gap between the walls began the path down the center of the glen, which was kept clean of animal unpleasantness by older children being punished for various crimes.

There was one thing this clan had that others did not. No one knew from where it came, but an edict had been handed down from generation to generation. It demanded death to any man who intentionally hurt a woman or a child and each new laird swore to uphold it, including Laird Justin MacGreagor.

Well aware of the dangers women faced and that word of his daughter's attractiveness seemed on the lips of many men, Justin encouraged Paisley to wear some sort of covering on her head when she went outside. She saw no difference between being the only one with white hair and the only one wearing a scarf in summer, but to please him she wore one that hung down to her waist. It matched her green shirt and the new plaid she pleated and tucked under the wide leather belt her brother made for her. Yet she was not partial to wearing any headscarf at all and on this day, she would not have to.

It was indeed a special time in the MacGreagor Glen.

The long summer days were hot and when the crops were finally gathered and the storehouse filled to the brim, the MacGreagors invited members of other clans to a feast.

The women prepared every kind of food including salted fish and beef, yellow carrots, onions, turnips, peas and cabbage. None spared the ginger, pepper, nutmeg and saffron used to please even the most finicky palate. Breads of every kind were made from ground barley, oats, rye and wheat, and at this time of year the feast offered grapes, cherries, plums, apples, nuts, fruit pies and sweet breads. It was a feast fit for kings, soon to be spread out on tables in the courtyard for all to enjoy.

While the women prepared the meal, the men set out the necessary equipment for games in the grasses of the glen. They drove a wooden spike in the ground, marked the appropriate number of paces away from it and set horseshoes in a row to mark the last step a man could take before the toss. Other men brought out wooden targets, some round and some square to determine the best with a bow and arrows, while still more made ready the skills of strength by hauling out heavy logs. In the game, the men first lifted the log with two hands, balanced it on one and made sure it did not tip to one side or the other. The one who could hold it there longer than any other man would be the winner and it was this skill that challenged the men most. Lighter logs gave those not yet fully grown an equal chance to show their skill.

At last, the guests arrived and the games began. For the better part of two hours the men tested their skills, the women applauded or jeered and a panel of three elders announced the winners. The little children played their normal games of Stones for the boys and Queen of Scots for the girls, while the older boys tested their skills by sparring with wooden swords.

Because it was so hot, Justin opened the front and back door allowing a cool breeze to blow through his large, three-story home, and seated his guests at the long table in his colorfully decorated great hall. Not much had changed in this room over the years. One wall displayed old and new weapons of every sort while tapestries adorned the other walls. The long table remained in the middle of the large room together with tall-backed chairs and well-stuffed pillows of every color for guests to sit on. A large hearth at one end kept the place warm in winter and a back door led to a kitchen.

Paisley was not surprised to find herself sitting between Laird Haldane and Laird Graham so she could help her father entertain his guests. She smiled often, sat up straight and paid as much attention to one laird as the other. She even leaned forward often to include Laird Haldane's wife in the conversation.

Normally on hot days, the women braided their hair and some even piled it on top of their heads, but Paisley was often cold when others were comfortable. She knew the feast would continue into the evening and left her uncovered hair down, except for two small braids on the sides that she tied together with a green string in the back.

Paisley was surprised by her reaction to Laird Chisholm Graham. Even though she had seen him during his occasional visits before, it was never up close and never in a circumstance where she could talk to him. She found him charming, his manners impeccable and his smile oddly exciting. The others at the table talked, and loudly so, but sometimes it was as if no one else was in the room.

Once, when she looked into his fascinating amber eyes a little too long, she forced her attention to his necklace. It was made of leather and the odd shaped square held a collection of rubies and emeralds, with one large diamond in the middle. He wore his shirt open a little at the neck to show off his jewels and before she realized what she was doing, she reached up, brushed her hand against his skin and turned the necklace toward her for a better look.

The hair on his chest was the same golden brown as that on his head and face, she noticed, but when Paisley realized she had touched a man not her husband, she was horrified. She let go of his necklace, avoided his eyes and began a conversation with Laird Haldane on the other side of her.

As soon as the meal was finished and the air cooled, Laird MacGreagor and his guests went outside to join in the celebration. To the tune of the flute player's music in the courtyard, two women tried to teach two men how to dance a new sort of jig and everyone roared with laughter. The men did not seem to mind, although they occasionally stopped to glare at one jeer or another from the crowd. It seemed a hopeless case, but the men kept right on trying and soon others joined and tried to learn.

Laird Graham was never very far away from her and it pleased Paisley. It seemed to please him too, but he was a handsome man, yet unmarried and probably sought after by any number of women. It was always so for a laird, even the unsightly ones and Chisholm Graham was anything but unsightly. Just now, however, he seemed to be all hers and she lavished in his company. When she drifted away to gain a better view of the dancers, he drifted with her and when she next had something to remark upon, he was near enough to hear her and respond.

They laughed together, rolled their eyes at the same time, and when Laird Graham suggested they sneak a slice of honey bread out from under the watchful eye of a woman determined not to let the children eat them all, she became a willing conspirator. It was not hard to do, for a handsome man was admired by all women, no matter her age, and while he distracted the unsuspecting woman, Paisley grabbed the slice, walked away and went to the other side of the crowd. Soon he was beside her, joined in her laughter and ate the stolen bread she shared with him.

For Paisley, it was the most glorious evening of her life. Too soon, the dancing ended, the visitors rode away and the MacGreagors settled down for a good night's sleep. Years before, the second floor of the three-story keep had been divided into two bedchambers and a sitting room, but with six children, the sitting room became another bedchamber for two of the boys. Paisley shared a room with her sister, Leslie, until Leslie married and now their bedchamber was all hers. Her father and mother occupied the third floor, but after Deora died giving birth to her sixth child, Justin hardly spent any time there. Her death was devastating to them all but in time he regained his good humor, as did his children.

Yet it was at times such as this, Paisley wished she could share the moment with her mother, or even her sister and perhaps stay up talking far into the night. Alas, Leslie had a husband and there was no one to talk to just now, so she looked out the window for a while longer and then went to bed.

LAIRD CHISHOLM GRAHAM lived less than an hour north of the MacGreagors and an easy path took him and his six-man guard across the river and through the narrow passageway between two hills. Once that was accomplished, the first of three well-traveled paths took him northwest toward home.

In the long days of summer, darkness fell for only a few hours a night, the horses knew the way and his men had consumed enough wine to make them less talkative.

Starting tomorrow, Chisholm guessed, his men would try lifting logs more often, so they could compete better the next time they were invited to join in the MacGreagor games. The thought made him smile. He remained considerably more sober than his men and with good reason—a man, even a laird, could not hope to impress the woman he found fascinating with slurred words and improper manners.

Her smiles and laughter greatly pleased him and it wasn't long before he decided he wanted to see those smiles and hear that laughter far more often. The question was: how long should he wait before he went back?

A WEEK LATER, LAIRD Graham had not come back and Paisley began to believe that instead of preferring her, he had only been pleasant for her father's sake.

Of her four younger brothers, one was far more enjoyable and sometimes far more bothersome than the other three. Justin named his eldest son Alisdair but the clan called him Sawney. He was the closest to her same age and seemed always to be in her way. Still, she was two years older and maintained at least a little control over him.

He was tall for his age and would likely be his father's same six feet, five inches by the time he was grown. He would look like Justin too, with dark hair and blue eyes, which would cause him to be sought after by women, if he ever managed to get beyond his awkward stage.

"God help the lass you marry," Paisley muttered as each step took them farther away from the village. Lately, Justin demanded that she not walk alone, even in the long, wide glen, for fear someone might take her, and this day, Sawney was her designated companion.

"I fear the same for your husband," Sawney said. He loved his sister and liked her too. She was often wise, usually even-tempered and did not mind answering his constant stream of questions. He saw nothing exceptional in her appearance, but if other men did, Sawney had no doubt she needed to be looked after. Every time he escorted her, it made him feel protective and all grown up.

"Sawney that is the third time you have bumped into me. Move over a pace or two."

He took two steps sideways and mockingly bowed. "As my lady wishes," he said in English instead of Gaelic.

Paisley rolled her eyes and kept walking. The spring flowers had come and gone, the morning was not yet too warm and the lower half of the glen held plenty of lush grass for their herd of horses to feed on. The cows grazed in an adjoining meadow and when she looked, the sheep were feasting on a faraway hillside.

Paisley's long shirt and pleated plaid were the same green as the trees in the forest except for the light blue threads woven between the green squares. On this day, she wore her matching scarf and new shoes that fit well.

"What, no argument?" Sawney asked. "Speaking English most often causes you great discomfort, though I cannot guess why."

She answered in English just to prove she could. "'Tis unnatural to speak it and I have yet to fully grasp why father makes us learn it still.

Mother was English and often needed help with Gaelic words, but now that she has passed, the teaching is useless."

"You are right, as usual."

Paisley stopped walking and suspiciously eyed her brother. "What are you up to?"

"Nothing, nothing at all. Someday we might have a need, but I have said that many times and I suspect you tire of hearing it." He was up to something and decided he might as well get it over with. Sawney was growing so fast, the bottom of his kilt barely touched his knees and soon he would need a new pair of shoes with straps long enough to lace up his calves. "Sister, do you wish to marry?"

"Well, I would like very much to live in a cottage instead of the Keep where I must walk past all the lads to go outside." She sighed. "Father will not allow it until I take a husband, therefore I must marry."

Sawney clasped his hands behind his back and started them walking again. "But you would not marry just any lad, would you?"

"I'd not marry the candle maker that is certain. Nor do I fancy a lad without humor, wit or one who does not favor me often with a pleasant smile."

"I have heard Thomas fancies you."

She wrinkled her brow. "Which one? We have three lads named Thomas and four named William. Are there not enough other names?"

"The Thomas I mention is a hunter and a very good one at that. You would do well to let him court you, for many a lass thinks him handsome."

"Some call you handsome as well, it means nothing."

Sawney wasn't certain if he should be flattered or insulted. As they walked, he often looked at the others in the glen until he was sure he recognized them, but Paisley wasn't in any real danger there. Although there were trees easy to hide behind on both sides, MacGreagor guards were posted at short intervals so they could notify the clan of strangers, wild boars or any other danger. Fortunately, there had been no whistles signaling danger in weeks.

Paisley glanced at the corral where the stallions were kept away from the mares, noticed all the men watching her and chose to leave the path in favor of a row of logs on the opposite side of the glen. It was near the graveyard but it was her best choice. At least dead men did not gawk.

Beyond a sister, a new brother-in-law and four brothers, she had four sets of aunts and uncles and enough cousins to make a clan of their own. "Brother, do you always want to live here? I mean, I often wish we could just ride away and find a new home."

He smiled. "I doubt it would help. A bonnie lass is a bonnie lass no matter where she is, and lads will always want to look at her."

She sat down on a log and folded her arms. "I am cursed."

"If you must pity someone, pity me for I am my father's eldest son."

"Do you fear becoming Laird someday?"

"Fear it, nay. All the same, Father regrets it and so did Grandfather, I am told." He lifted his right foot and rested it on top of the log.

"If that be the case, once I am married we will encourage Father to ask the clan to choose another laird. Then he and all four of his sons can live in a small cottage like the rest of the people. Would you find that to your liking?"

"To spend more time with Father, I would live in a cart."

Paisley giggled. "Done then...as soon as I marry."

He returned her mischievous grin. "What shall Father become; a hunter, a guard or perhaps a tanner of hides?"

"I say we let him get his fill of fishing first. 'Tis that he loves most."

"As do I. An entire day fishing with Father without interruption, would be a dream come true, even if he demands we take my brothers with us."

"Would he truly relent though? I..."

Just then, a faint whistle at the small end of the glen interrupted them.

"Strangers," said Sawney. He stood up straight and reached out his hand. "To the forest, my lady." As soon as she got up, he hurried her across the graveyard, through the thick bushes and into the trees. Then they both laughed and relaxed.

Approaching strangers was not an uncommon occurrence, especially now with all the gossip about Paisley. At first, her father allowed men to meet her, but lately Justin wanted none of them to see her and Paisley was beginning to spend more time in hiding than anywhere else. Even when the women went to bathe in the loch, he dared not let her go. Instead, she used the bathing basin brought some years past from England. Nevertheless, she loved to swim and even the privilege of bathing in private seemed just another place to hide.

Often, when more than one red deer was shot, the meat was placed in a pit, slow cooked for days and then shared by the entire clan. Herbs and spices made the otherwise tough meat tender, wine washed it down and the meal was again followed by dancing and singing to the music of the flute player. It was something they all looked forward to and the aroma that filled the air just now made Paisley hungry.

She did not care to even look at the strangers and assumed these were just more of the sort that came to gawk at her. What her father said to send them on their way, she did not know, nor did she care. They would be gone soon enough and that was all that mattered.

Careful to stay hidden, she leaned down, picked a forest flower and stood back up. Then she smelled it, peeked around the tree and caught her breath. The strangers numbered over twenty, a laird and his guard all dressed in matching white shirts with dark blue kilts. Each held his head high, rode his mount with pride and kept his weapons sheathed. Dark blue and white were the colors of the Grahams and when the man in the middle turned his face her way, her eyes lit up. "'Tis Laird Graham, he has come back!"

"So he has," said Sawney. The excitement in her voice was not lost on him and he suspected his friend, Thomas, would soon be sadly refused. Oh well, MacGreagor women were allowed to choose their own husbands and as painful as it was for MacGreagor men, that was the way it was.

She watched Chisholm ride all the way into the courtyard, dismount and go inside to greet her father. His return did not mean he preferred her and she was not sure if she should stay hidden, wait for Justin to send for her, or walk back into the glen where Laird Graham might easily find her.

Suddenly, an arm went around Paisley's waist, a hand clamped over her mouth and her eyes widened in horror. She dropped the flower and looked at Sawney, but he had troubles of his own. A second man had a firm grip on him and held the blade of a dagger to her brother's throat. She struggled to free her hand enough to pull her dagger, but when the man threatened to kill Sawney, she begrudgingly relaxed.

A second later, her attacker lifted her off the ground, hauled her up the hill and then hurried down the other side. Once they got to a horse, he abruptly let go of her, turned her around, hit her hard under the chin and knocked her out. Then he laid her over the back of the horse, untied the reins, mounted behind her and raced through the trees.

"LADDIE, DO NOT TURN around or I will cut you ear to ear," the husky voice said in Sawney's ear.

For agonizing seconds, the older, stronger man kept his grip around Sawney's upper torso pinning his arms to his sides. Sawney could hear Paisley being taken away and had to do something even if it was wrong. He mustered all his strength, quickly put his right foot between his attacker's and looped it around a leg. Then he pulled hard. The warrior released him to regain his balance, stumbled and then fell on his backside. Sawney drew his sword as he spun around and quickly put the tip of it to the middle of the stranger's neck.

His eyes filled with rage and he wanted to kill the man. Instead, he put two fingers to his mouth and gave off the long, shrill whistle signaling danger. Not far away, a MacGreagor guard raced to his side and drew his own sword.

"Watch him, a lad took Paisley!"

"Sawney, you are bleeding!" Neasan shouted.

At a dead run, Sawney headed up the hillside and disappeared over the top, but by then, the man and Paisley were gone.

End of sample chapter.

Pick up your copy of this book today!

More Marti Talbott Books

www.martitalbott.com

To discover free Marti Talbott books and more historical novels filled with castles and kings, love and war, triumph and tribulation - click here[1].

Follow Clan MacGreagor through multiple generations beginning with *The Viking*[2] where it all began, *The Highlanders*[3] and their struggle to survive, *Marblestone Mansion*[4] and the duke who simply could not get rid of his scandalous duchess, and still more historical stories in *The Lost MacGreagor Books*[5]. Then check out **Marti's contemporary romance/mysteries**[6] in *Missing Heiress, Greed and a Mistress, The Dead Letters*, and *The Locked Room*. Other books include the **Carson Series**[7], *Leanna, (a short story)*, and **Seattle Quake 9.2**[8].

See what's Marti's working on next and sign up to be notified when it is released.[9]

Marti's Website[10] Talk to Marti on Facebook[11]

---

1. http://www.martitalbott.com

2. http://www.martitalbott.com/viking-series

3. http://www.martitalbott.com/highlander-series

4. http://www.martitalbott.com/marblestone-mansion

5. http://www.martitalbott.com/The-Lost-MacGreagor-Books

6. http://www.martitalbott.com/m-t-romance

7. http://www.martitalbott.com/the-carson-series

8. http://www.martitalbott.com/more-marti-talbott-books

9. http://www.martitalbott.com/Home/notify-me

10. http://www.martitalbott.com

11. https://www.facebook.com/marti.talbot

Made in the USA
Coppell, TX
01 December 2019